Rebecca cherishes Andy's friendship now more than ever before.

Rebecca Sutherland sat in the back row holding Andy's hand. "I don't know if I can go through with this," she whispered. "I've never been face-to-face with Dick since he was arrested."

"When you testify don't think about Dick, think about Anita and the two children. Remember, this is not your decision. Your only responsibility is to tell the facts as you know them and leave the rest up to the judge and jury."

Rebecca grinned as she squeezed her friend's hand. "Thanks. I needed that. I'm glad you'll be by my side during this entire ordeal to give me moral support."

Suddenly the side door opened and the bailiff entered the courtroom. "Please rise," he ordered. "The District Court of Cascade County is now in session. The Honorable Herman Kessler presiding."

As soon as Judge Kessler took his seat on the bench, he pounded his gavel and commanded. "You may be seated. The court will come to order." He paused. "The clerk will call the first case."

The clerk rose and monotoned. "The State of Montana versus Richard Reed."

"Mr. Reed," the judge said. "You are charged with three counts of murder in the first degree."

ANN BELL, a librarian by profession, lives in Billings, Montana, with her attorney husband. Ann has worked as a teacher and librarian in schools in Iowa, Oregon, Guam, as well as Montana. Previously she has written numerous articles for Christian magazines and a book titled *Proving Yourself: A Study of James.*

Books by Ann Bell

HEARTSONG PRESENTS
HP66—Autumn Love
HP89—Contagious Love
HP109—Inspired Love

Distant Love

Ann Bell

Rocky Bluff Chronicles

Heartsong Presents

This book is dedicated to the gallant people of Guam
who during World War II endured three years
of a brutal Japanese military occupation but never once lost
their faith in God and the United States of America.

A note from the Author:
*I love to hear from my readers! You may write to me at the following
address:*

> Ann Bell
> Author Relations
> P.O. Box 719
> Uhrichsville, OH 44683

ISBN 1-55748-765-0

DISTANT LOVE

PRINTED IN THE U.S.A.

one

"Help me, someone please help me!"

Rebecca Sutherland bolted upright in bed. *Am I dreaming or is someone actually calling for help?* The pounding on the front door continued along with the intermittent ringing of the door bell.

"Fire. . . Fire. . . My house is on fire. My wife and children are inside. Please help me."

Rebecca grabbed her robe from the foot of the bed as she ran to the front door. She flung open the door. There stood Dick Reed barefoot, dressed only in a pair of boxer shorts. A red glow radiated from the house next door.

"Rebecca, call the fire department! Anita and the kids are still inside."

Rebecca rushed to the phone and dialed 9-1-1.

"Emergency Services. May I help you?"

"There's a fire at the Dick Reed residence, Twenty-Five Fifteen Rimrock Road. The wife and four children are still inside," Rebecca panted.

"The fire trucks and ambulance will be right there," the dispatcher assured her. "Try to remain calm until they arrive."

Rebecca ran outside. Dick was just coming around the side of the house with four-year-old Donna in one arm and two-year-old Jackie in the other. Pat Crouse came running across the street with her robe wrapped loosely around her. Sirens could be heard in the distance. Flames were now leaping from the windows of the Reed home.

Pat took the two children from their father's arms while Rebecca tried to comfort her next door neighbor. "I've got to go back," Dick shouted as he turned back toward the house. "Anita, Chris, and the baby are still in there."

Rebecca held his shoulder. "The fire's spread throughout the house," she stated firmly. "The fire trucks are on their way. They'll get them out for you."

The fire truck screeched to a stop in front of the Reed home and eight firemen began running hoses to the nearby fire hydrant. The fire chief's car stopped behind the truck and the ambulance parked behind him. The neighborhood was a flurry of activity. Additional volunteer firemen appeared in pick-up trucks from all directions.

The cool mountain breeze enveloped Fire Chief Andrew Hatfield as he quickly approached the small band huddled by the curb. "Dick, who's left in the house?"

"My wife, Anita, six-year-old Chris, and the baby."

"What rooms did you last see them in?"

Dick bit his lip. "Anita was asleep in the master bedroom and the baby was in a bassinet in the corner of the room. Chris was asleep in the room across the hall."

"We'll get them out," Chief Hatfield assured him and then turned his attention to Rebecca. "Mrs. Sutherland, would you take Dick and the children to your house and warm them up? Could we use your place as a command post for a few hours?"

"Certainly," Rebecca replied. "I'll put on a large coffee pot for anyone who needs to get out of this wind."

"Dick, we'll let you know just as soon as we locate the rest of your family," Chief Hatfield assured him. "We have the ambulance standing by and have notified Med-Evac from Great Falls. They'll have their helicopters land in the school parking lot where they can be transferred to the

Burn Center, if necessary. All you can do now is go with Rebecca and wait and pray."

Rebecca put her arm around Dick and directed him toward her front door. The tranquility of the living room conflicted with the terror and confusion outside. Pat sat the two stunned toddlers on the sofa and reached for the afghan to wrap around Jackie's trembling body. Rebecca grabbed another blanket from the hall closet for Donna.

"Dick," Rebecca said as she hugged Donna against her chest. "I'm sorry this house is devoid of men's clothes, but I do have a sloppy pair of sweats that might be big enough to fit you."

"Anything'll be fine," Dick mumbled as he slumped into the recliner. "I wish they'd hurry and tell me something. They should've found them by now."

Rebecca handed Donna to Pat as she hurried to the bedroom. "Is Mommy going to be okay?" the child sobbed.

"The firemen are working as fast as they can," Pat assured her as she cuddled the two children. "Why don't you and Jackie stretch out on the sofa and try to get some sleep? We'll let you know how they are as soon as we know."

Donna pulled her two-year-old sister close to her as she put her head on a pillow and straightened her legs. She sobbed softly as she watched Jackie close her eyes.

Rebecca returned to the living room carrying a pair of faded gray sweats and handed them to her neighbor. The warmth of the clothing felt good to Dick as he pulled them over his shivering body and slumped into the recliner.

"I better get the coffee pot started," Rebecca stated as she hurried to the kitchen. "Dick, can I make you a cup of instant while the pot's brewing?"

"I'm fine," Dick muttered as he stared nervously out the

window at the activity next door.

Pat went to the window. "It looks like they're getting the fire under control. I'm sure we'll be hearing something soon."

"I hope so," Dick muttered. "This night seems like an eternity."

Pat had just returned to the sofa where the children were sleeping when the doorbell rang. She hurried to the door and flung it open. There stood Police Captain Philip Mooney holding a small bundle. "Any news?" she begged.

"The firemen kicked in the door to the back porch and found the kitten. I thought the children would like to cuddle it as they wait," the officer explained as Donna let go of her sleeping sister and hurried to retrieve her pet.

"How's my mommy?" Donna begged as she cuddled her kitten.

Captain Mooney knelt before the child. "We haven't found them yet, but it shouldn't be long now. Will you take care of the kitten while we keep looking?"

Donna nodded and then took the kitten back to the sofa where her sister was beginning to stir. "Look Jackie. They found Muffie."

Just then Rebecca appeared from the kitchen and nodded to the officer. "How's it going?"

"We haven't found them yet," Phil Mooney replied. "This is the worst tragedy I've seen in my life. The night Harkness Hardware Store burned was bad enough, but at least lives weren't involved there."

Dick appeared detached from the tragedy going on around him when Captain Mooney approached the recliner by the window. "I'm sorry for what is happening. I wish we could do more. Chief Hatfield will be by shortly to talk with you."

"I appreciate your concern," Dick replied with a glaze in his eyes. "I know you're doing all you can."

No sooner had Captain Mooney left than the fire chief arrived at Rebecca's door. He greeted everyone and then pulled a chair close to Dick.

"I'm sorry, Dick. We did the best we could, but the flames were too hot by the time we arrived. We found your wife by the children's window, the matting on the baby's bassinet melted and the baby fell through to the floor. We found the older child's body in the hallway. He must have been trying to escape by himself. Our first observations are that Anita broke the window and got the first two children out but was overcome with smoke when she turned to get the other two. Where were you when the fire broke out?"

A long silence enveloped the room. Dick's eyes became even more glazed than before. "I. . .I. . .I was in the living room watching TV," he mumbled. "I must have fallen asleep on the sofa because when I awoke the house was full of smoke and flames were coming from the hallway. I didn't know what to do so I came to get Rebecca."

Chief Hatfield cleared his throat. "The bodies are being taken to the hospital for autopsy. You'll need to select a mortuary to handle the final arrangements," he said. I'll have more questions in the morning after we've begun to investigate the cause of the fire. In the meantime, if there's anything we can do please feel free to call." Chief Hatfield shook Dick's hand and started for the doorway. He paused as he noticed Rebecca standing in the kitchen doorway dressed in a royal blue robe, her hair tousled around her face.

"Rebecca, may I speak to you privately in the kitchen," the fire chief asked.

"Certainly," she responded as she led the graying career fireman into the kitchen and pointed to a chair by the window. "Would you care for a cup of coffee?"

"I'd appreciate one. It's been a long night and I'm afraid it's going to get even longer," Chief Hatfield sighed as he slumped into a chair. "There's a lot of suspicious loose ends about this fire."

"How's that?" Rebecca queried as she poured two mugs of coffee.

"Don't you think it's pretty unusual that Dick would come to your home before he tried to get his family out of the fire?"

Rebecca sat in a chair across the fire chief. She was still shaking, she noticed, but she made herself choke back the sorrow and horror she felt about Anita and the two children who had not escaped the fire. She took a sip of coffee. "That bothered me from the beginning, but he said the fire was so intense in the hallway and he was frightened and couldn't think straight. I took that explanation at face value."

"I guess I have a suspicious mind," Chief Hatfield confessed, "but my years in investigative work have taught me to question everything. Tonight after things settle down, would you jot down every observation and impression you had from the moment you first heard pounding on your front door? I'll be by tomorrow and take a complete statement. The arson investigation will begin just as soon as it is light."

"You don't think Dick actually started the fire, do you?"

"I'm not making any accusations at this point," Chief Hatfield stated. "I'm merely trying to make a thorough investigation as to the cause of the fire. Thank's for all the help you've been. I'd better get out there and see how the clean-up is progressing. I'll see you tomorrow."

Her haze of grief parted for a moment, and a puzzled expression covered Rebecca's face as she followed the fire chief to the door. She closed the door behind him and turned to the dazed father sitting in the corner.

"Dick, I suppose you'll be wanting to make some phone calls."

"I guess I'd better give Anita's family a call, but my address book burned in the fire," Dick mumbled as he followed Rebecca to the kitchen phone. "They live in Spokane."

"What's her father's name? I'll call directory assistance for you."

"Kenneth Taylor. Her mother's name is Laura. Kenneth has a bad heart so I hope the shock won't be too hard on him."

Rebecca dialed directory assistance for the Spokane area and wrote the number on scratch paper. She dialed the number and waited. When the phone began to ring on the other end she handed the receiver to Dick and left the room. This was a time when he would need privacy the most.

The former librarian of Rocky Bluff High School returned to the living room and sat in the chair next to her neighbor. "I'm glad to see the children finally went to sleep," she whispered. "When Dick gets off the phone I'll see if he wants to get some rest in the guest room. We're going to have a long few days."

"It's a good thing tomorrow's Saturday and I'm off work," Pat replied. "I'll begin getting community assistance organized. I assume Dick will want to stay at his motel with the children until he's able to find another place."

"Perhaps," Rebecca replied. "But for the next few days they're more than welcome to stay here. He's going to need a lot of help caring for the children while making the final arrangements for Anita and the other two children. He must be numb with grief."

Pat wiped the tears from her eyes. "It's such a tragedy. They were the model family. They built the Sleepy-Eye Motel from a depressing flop-house to the nicest motel in town. They both were so devoted to their children."

"That's what bothers me," Rebecca replied. "Why didn't he try to get his family out before he came here to report the fire?"

Pat's eyes widened and then she shrugged her shoulders. "I guess one never knows how they might react under pressure," she sighed.

"Pat, why don't you go on home and get some rest," Rebecca said as she patted her friend on the arm. "I'm going to be depending a lot on you during the next few days."

"Are you sure there's nothing else I can help you with before I leave?"

"No. I think I've poured the last cup of coffee for the evening and I'm sure Dick will want to get some rest as soon as he finishes calling relatives."

Dick insisted on the two children sleeping with him so Rebecca carried Jackie while Dick carried Donna into the guest room. He thanked her for her hospitality and closed the door. Rebecca returned to her bedroom and collapsed onto her pillow. She tossed and turned the remainder of the night without ever completely returning to sleep. When the sun began to shine through the closed blinds, Rebecca arose. She showered and then began brewing a fresh pot of coffee and fixing herself a couple pieces of toast.

As she was spreading the strawberry jam on her toast the doorbell rang. She laid the knife on the corner of the plate and hurried to the front door. "Chief Hatfield, do come in."

"I'm sorry I'm so early, but the investigation team rolled into action at dawn. They're next door right now securing the premises."

"No problem," Rebecca assured him. "Can I pour you a cup of coffee and fix you a bite to eat?"

"I'd appreciate that," he grinned as he eyed her plate. "Do you have a couple more pieces of bread to slap in the toaster?"

"Chief Hatfield, it'd be a pleasure," she responded, trying to mask the fatigue and strain of the night before.

"To you it's Andy," he chuckled and then became serious. "Are your guests still sleeping?"

"I haven't heard any stirring coming from that room since I've been up," Rebecca replied as she hurriedly set another place at the table and poured a cup of coffee.

Andy shook his head with approval. "Good, because I think we have a real tiger by the tail. This investigation is becoming more and more suspicious and I'm going to be depending on your observations a great deal to provide us with possible leads."

"I'll help all I can," Rebecca promised, "but I'm afraid I haven't noticed anything out of the ordinary. Dick talked with his wife's parents for quite a while last night. Anita's parents and her sister and husband are flying in this afternoon from Spokane. They'll be staying with Pat Crouse for a few days while the Taylors will probably stay with Edith Dutton."

Andy wrinkled his brow. "Why don't they all stay at the motel?"

Rebecca shrugged her shoulders. "Dick said it would be too hard for them to stay in the motel that he and Anita worked so hard to build."

Andy's expression softened as he eyed the middle-aged librarian across the table. "The strain of this is going to be hard for the next few days. Are you sure you want to be headquarters for all the commotion?"

"I think I'm up to it," Rebecca assured him. "Besides, the first of August I'm leaving for a two week vacation in Hawaii before I go on to Guam and my new job. I'll just leave Rocky Bluff with a blaze of excitement."

"That it will be," Andy replied. "I brought my tape recorder along to begin taking your statement as to the events of last night. If Dick gets up we'll have to stop and continue another time. However, your first impressions are crucial to the investigation."

For the next hour and a half Andy questioned Rebecca concerning every detail of the events of the night before. She answered the best she could, but the stress of the ordeal was beginning to take its toll. Her voice faltered. Andy's concern for her mental stress became apparent as he sat in silence while Rebecca stared out the kitchen window.

I haven't had any personal contact with Andy since he moved to Rocky Bluff five years ago and yet there is something familiar about him, Rebecca mused. *I wonder who he reminds me of?*

Rebecca's thoughts drifted back through the years. She had grown up in a little town in Iowa and had gotten her teaching degree from the University of Northern Iowa. Two weeks after graduation she married Eric Sutherland and moved to Mason City, Iowa, where he was the social studies teacher and she was the school librarian. Everything was going well for them and they were making plans to start a family in a couple of years. However, the Vietnam War was at its peak and Eric's number was drawn in the lottery for military service. Within months Eric was a First Lieutenant in the United States Army and leading a platoon in the Tet Offensive.

After she was notified of his death she stayed in Mason City for a couple more years, but could not shake loose his memory. Rebecca sold their small home in Mason City and accepted a position as the high school librarian in Rocky Bluff, Montana. Using part of his insurance money, Rebecca bought one of the nicer homes there. Since she was certain she would never be able to fall in love again, her home, school, and church became a replacement for intimate relationships. No one would ever be able to match the pedestal her war hero had been placed upon.

Rebecca visualized Eric's warm compassionate eyes and suddenly saw that same compassion in Andy's eyes. *I wonder if Eric would look like that today?* she pondered. *Would he have distinguished gray hair or would his hair have thinned and left him bald?*

"Rebecca, I know you're getting tired," Chief Hatfield said as her faraway gaze prolonged. "Why don't I come back later today after you've had time to rest."

"I'm sorry," she replied. "I'm having trouble keeping my mind on task. Maybe I'll be able to remember more after I've rested. I certainly hope you can complete the investigation soon."

Suddenly Jackie's cry could be heard from the guest room and then Dick's low voice trying to comfort her. "I'd better be going. At this point the less Dick knows the better off the investigation will be."

Rebecca escorted the fire chief to the door and then returned to her private thoughts. *The terror of last night is bad enough, but why do the memories of thirty years ago come back and haunt me now?*

two

"There's Grandma and Grandpa," four-year-old Donna shouted as the distraught couple emerged from the Treasure State Airlines landing gate. She released her daddy's hand and ran to her grandfather who picked her up and hugged her tight.

Tears built in his eyes. "How are you doing, sweetheart?"

"I miss my mommy," she sobbed. "Our house burnt down last night and she went to heaven."

"I know," Ken Taylor choked. "We came to say goodbye to her along with Chris and the baby."

Laura Taylor hesitantly approached her son-in-law. "Dick, how are you holding up?"

"Not well, but the people of Rocky Bluff are being extremely supportive." Dick forced a weak smile. "I'm staying next door with Rebecca Sutherland, the high school librarian. I can't bear the thought of going to the motel where Anita worked so hard."

"We feel the same way," Ken replied. "We don't think we'll be able to go near the motel nor the burned-out house."

"One of the elderly women of the church has offered to let you stay with her. Her husband's in the nursing home and she complains that her home is too large for just her," Dick replied. "She's an absolute jewel. Her name's Edith Dutton."

"That's one advantage of a small town," Laura sighed. "Spokane has lost the neighbor-helping-neighbor environment. We scarcely know those who live in the same apartment complex."

"Everyone's been so good to us. Several women have already begun gathering clothing and household goods for us." Dick paused and the distressed family began to move slowly toward the baggage claim. "I have an appointment with the funeral director and the pastor later this afternoon to make funeral arrangements. Would you like to join me?"

Laura gulped. "I'd appreciate that. It's the least I can do for our beloved Anita."

"I'll take you to Edith's so you can settle in and then come back and get you at three o'clock."

The Taylors clung to their grandchildren as their son-in-law drove the familiar streets of Rocky Bluff. Within twenty minutes Dick, his daughters, and his in-laws were ringing Edith Dutton's doorbell.

"Welcome," Edith greeted. "Do come in."

"Edith, I'd like you to meet Anita's parents, Kenneth and Laura Taylor. Ken and Laura, this is Edith Dutton. She's been an inspiration and comfort to the entire town."

Laura reached out and took Edith's hand. "We appreciate you opening your home to us. With Anita's love and hard work in the motel business it's too painful for us to stay in such a cold environment."

"I understand only too well," Edith replied as she squeezed the grieving mother's hand. "You're welcome to stay here for as long as you need."

"Thank you. We appreciate your thoughtfulness," Laura said as she wiped a tear from her eye. "The town seems to be doing everything possible to help."

"It was such a shock to us all, " Edith replied. "I only wish there were more we could do."

Up to that moment Dick had been standing restlessly in

the entryway. "If you would excuse me for a little while, I'd like to take the girls back to Rebecca's and rest. I don't think I got any sleep at all last night."

"Daddy, can I stay with Grandma?" Donna begged as she wrapped her arms around her grandmother.

Dick looked at his mother-in-law who nodded her head with approval. "If you'd like. I'll be back in an hour so we can go to the funeral home."

As soon as Dick left with two-year-old Jackie, Donna crawled into her grandmother's lap and sobbed. Laura held her tight as she shared her grief.

Tears gathered in Edith's eyes as she watched the two.

Gradually Donna's sobs subsided. "Mommy and Daddy had a big fight last night. They yelled a lot. Mommy said she wanted to take us and come and live with you."

Everyone's face blanched as they exchanged questioning glances. *Surely nothing suspicious happened,* Edith mused, *but there are so many details that don't add up.*

Laura masked her suspicions as she tried to comfort her granddaughter. "Maybe after the funeral you and Jackie can come stay with us. Your mother's old room has been empty ever since she grew up."

"We don't have any place to live here," Donna replied somberly. "Will Daddy come too?"

Laura exchanged glances with her husband. "Probably not for a while. He still has the motel to take care of."

To break the tension, Edith showed Laura to the guest room and invited her to unpack. Stretching out on the bed did little to relax the grieving couple.

As promised Dick returned within an hour. "That short nap certainly helped me," he stated as he surveyed his weary in-laws. "Are you ready to go?"

The Taylors bade Edith good-bye and followed Dick to

his waiting car with Donna clinging tightly to her grandmother's hand. A sense of terror enveloped them. Would they be able to view their only daughter's body lying in a casket with two of her children in tiny caskets beside her?

ॐ

Rebecca had several things she wanted to get done, but her body wanted to sleep. It took several chimes from the doorbell before she was fully awake. She rubbed her hands over her hair and hurried to the front door.

"Chief Hatfield, do come in."

"I hope I didn't come at an inappropriate time. I knew that Dick was going to be at the funeral home late this afternoon and I wanted to talk to you when he wasn't here."

"He's planning to spend the evening with his in-laws and probably won't be back until bedtime. Chief Hatfield, please have a seat. Can I get you a cup of coffee?"

"I'd love a cup, but please call me Andy."

Rebecca rushed to the kitchen and poured two cups of coffee and arranged a half dozen homemade cookies on a dessert plate. Within five minutes she joined the fire chief at the other end of the sofa.

Andy took a long sip of his coffee and a bite of cookie before he spoke. "Rebecca, how would you evaluate Dick and Anita's marriage?"

Rebecca hesitated. She gazed out the window toward the charred house next door. "On the surface they appeared like a model, hardworking family, but occasionally I sensed some unrest underneath."

"How's that?"

"Well. . . On cool evenings when I'd turn off the air conditioner and open the windows, I often heard angry shouts, but I passed them off as normal family squabbles."

"Did you hear anything specific?" Andy cleared his throat. "Threats or the like?"

"Not really. The exact words were not distinct. However, once I did hear her shout 'Why do you hate me so?'"

Andy's eyes widened. "Did you hear a response?"

"I didn't pay much attention," Rebecca replied, "but I do remember hearing him say that she was an albatross around his neck and that he could go a long way in life without her."

"Do you have any idea why he came to your door without first trying to get his family out?" Andy queried.

Rebecca shook her head. "I've asked myself that repeatedly and can't come up with a good explanation. Dick said he was sleeping on the sofa and when he awoke the heat was too intense to get down the hallway to the children's bedroom."

"That's what he told us last night, but somehow the excuse just doesn't ring true. Although now I only have a gut level feeling."

"It sounds awfully suspicious to me too, but I can't put my finger on anything specific. Maybe I've watched too many TV mysteries."

The couple went over what seemed like every conceivable detail of the night before, but were unable to come to any conclusion. The sun was setting before Andy finished his interview with Rebecca.

Andy looked at her tired eyes. "I appreciate all the help you've been. The least I can do is treat you to dinner at Beefy's Steak House. I'm sure the last thing you want to do is prepare a meal for yourself."

"I was planning on heating up a TV dinner, but the Steak House sounds a lot tastier. However, I'll have to warn you that I'm too tired to be reasonable company."

"That's okay," Andy grinned. "I won't be the life of the party myself."

As the evening progressed the table conversation between Andy and Rebecca was limited but a nonverbal bond developed. Each had the maturity to relax and accept the other's fatigue without further social demands. After the final bite of dessert and the last sip of coffee were enjoyed Andy drove Rebecca home and walked her to her door.

"Our evening dialogue may not have been the most exciting," Rebecca concluded with a smile, "but I feel a lot was said in our silence."

Andy gave her hand a squeeze. "I feel much the same way. After this case is settled, maybe we can get together under more desirable circumstances."

Rebecca's smile became even broader. "I'd like that, but right now a good night's sleep is my highest priority."

❧

Donna and Jackie Reed fell into an exhausted sleep on the makeshift beds that Edith Dutton had prepared for them in the corner of her living room. Ken Taylor turned to his son-in-law.

"Dick, Laura and I have been talking. It's going to be several weeks before you'll be able to get settled again so we'd like to take the girls back to Spokane with us after the funeral."

Laura held her breath expecting a near violent objection from Dick. Instead a mysterious sense of relief came over him. "Yes. I suppose you're right. It'll take me a while to find another place to live. The motel is no place to keep two small children for very long."

"Tomorrow we can go shopping and get a minimum wardrobe for them and buy the rest when we get back to Spokane," Laura suggested.

"A couple of the ladies have been collecting clothing, toys, and household goods for the Reeds," Edith explained, hoping to alleviate some of the tension that hung over the room. "Tomorrow maybe you'd like to stop at Pat Crouse's and see what fits them. I was talking with Teresa Lennon while you were out and she said the community response has been overwhelming. Pat's basement is nearly full of donations."

"I don't like being considered a charity case," Dick retorted. "I do have a profitable business, I want you to know."

Edith gulped and took a deep breath. "Everyone's aware of that. They just want to help. They thought the world of Anita and the kids and they wanted to help make the transition through this difficult time as easy as possible."

Dick focused his eyes through the window onto the neighbor's roof. "I suppose you're right. I don't have anything to dress the girls in. Could you meet me at Pat's around ten-thirty tomorrow?"

"No problem," Ken responded briskly.

Dick eyed his sleeping children on the floor. "I need to go and get some rest, but they're sleeping so soundly. I hate to awaken them," Dick yawned. "Laura, would you mind watching them tonight and bring them to me at Rebecca's in the morning?"

"I'd be glad to," the children's grandmother replied. "They look like such sleeping angels now. Yet they've been through so much."

As Dick slipped out of Edith Dutton's front door into the darkening skies, Ken's face reddened. "There's something wrong here. That boy's acting awfully strange after just losing his wife and two children."

Edith shook her head. "I don't know what to think," she

sighed. "I know people react differently during crisis situations. But in all the years I've known the Reeds I've never seen Dick so detached from what's going on around him."

&

Storm clouds hung heavy over Rocky Bluff as the town's people crowded into the church to say farewell to Anita Reed and little Christopher and Ricky. Before the service the family gathered in the basement. Relatives from several states who had not seen each other in years greeted each other with unashamed tears.

Upstairs Rebecca Sutherland slid into the pew next to Edith Dutton. "Hello," she whispered. "How are you doing?"

"It's such a difficult time," Edith whispered back. "I'm so glad I could be hostess to the Taylors. They're such delightful people and are so grief stricken."

"After meeting them I can understand where Anita got her strength of character," Rebecca responded. "It's too bad that her life had to be cut short before she could reach her full potential."

Fire Chief Hatfield slipped quietly into the seat next to Rebecca just as Pastor Rhodes stepped to the pulpit. The two exchanged nods of greeting and then turned their attention to the front of the church.

"May the peace of God be with you," Pastor Rhodes began as the soft organ music trailed into the background. His words of comfort and encouragement taken from the Bible helped lift the troubled spirit that enveloped the congregation that Friday morning. The vocal music continued to remind the mourners of God's promise of a better life after death.

After the service first the family and then the rest of the mourners filed out of the church and proceeded to Pine

Hill Memorial Cemetery. "Would you two ladies like a ride to the cemetery?" Andy asked as he turned his attention back to Rebecca and Edith.

"Thanks for the offer," Rebecca replied. "We'd appreciate it."

Edith nodded her approval. "I hate to impose, but I can no longer drive myself."

"That's why we're a community," Andy replied as he put his arm on her shoulder. "You've done your part by providing housing for Anita's parents."

A faint smile crossed Edith's face. "I think they were more of an encouragement to me than I was to them."

Andy showed the women to his car and then waited his turn to join the procession. At the cemetery he offered his arm to Edith as they walked to the gravesite over the loose gravel path. Rebecca, who was a little more sure-footed, followed closely behind.

After everyone had gathered, Pastor Rhodes gave the final benediction for the lives of three young people that ended prematurely. Donna Reed clung tightly to her grandmother's hand while Dick held two-year-old Jackie. "Grandma, do we have to leave Mommy here in the cold ground alone?" Donna cried. "I want to stay with her."

Laura Taylor knelt before her granddaughter and took her in her arms. "Honey, only your mother's body is in that box. She's in heaven with Jesus now. Someday we'll all go to be with her and the entire family will be together again."

Just then the sun began to move from behind the clouds in the southern sky. The rays that descended appeared as rays of hope to the mourners as they departed the cemetery.

After Andy drove the two women back to the church to

get Rebecca's car, the two longtime friends decided on having lunch at Bea's Restaurant. While waiting for the waitress to bring their sandwiches, Rebecca turned to Edith.

"How did you ever handle retiring so easily? I'm having all kinds of problems accepting the fact that I won't be returning to Rocky Bluff High School next year, although I'm looking forward to my two year adventure on Guam."

Edith chuckled. "You're looking at me as a model of accepting retirement? I left the high school mentally kicking and screaming all the way."

"It didn't appear that way to the rest of us," Rebecca replied. "You always seemed so gracious and composed."

"It wasn't until I had a heart attack that I fully accepted the fact that my life would never be the same again." Edith smiled as she placed her napkin on her lap. "Now I'm enjoying my independence from the seven to four routine more than teaching. The only thing I miss is not having Roy home with me. It's difficult only being able to spend a few hours a day with him at the nursing home."

"I feel like a new high school graduate," Rebecca said. "Everything I'm familiar with is behind me and a strange unknown beckons."

Edith chuckled. "That's a poetic way to put it."

Rebecca stared out the window and the passing traffic. "To be honest," she finally admitted. "I'm afraid of growing old alone. Up until now I've immersed myself in Rocky Bluff High School, but now that period is over. You at least found Roy to share your life with after you retired. I'm too set in my ways to share my life with anyone."

"After George died I accepted the fact that I would never remarry. I certainly didn't go out and look for love, it just happened as an added blessing in my life," Edith explained with a peaceful smile. "One never knows the twists and turns her life may take. I'm just glad we have a God who guides and comforts us through all the hills and valleys. These last few days have been a pretty deep valley, but the happiness from our shared love gives us strength to continue on."

The waitress set two plates of French dip sandwiches before the women. They nodded their appreciation and returned to their private conversation.

"I'll have to rely on the shared love with the people of Rocky Bluff while I'm alone on Guam," Rebecca admitted. "I have such mixed emotions about going. I'm both excited and fearful."

"It sounds like a wonderful adventure," Edith replied. "If Roy and I were ten years younger we'd probably join you. My motto has always been to live each moment to the maximum."

three

Chief Hatfield leaned back in his chair and stretched his legs. "Rebecca, I hope you've recuperated from your week of helping the Reeds."

"I'm beginning to get caught up on my sleep," she sighed. "But everytime I go outside and look at the charred house all I can think about is Anita and the children."

Andy smiled at the middle-aged woman across the table. "I know that must be difficult. Maybe it's a good thing you'll be leaving soon for Guam. A different environment will help erase the nightmare of that night."

"I hope so," Rebecca agreed. "All the arrangements are made. I have a real nice couple moving into this house next week. I suppose you know Dan and Beth Blair."

"Oh, yes. He's the director of the crisis center. I've heard a lot of good things about his work. He took over the directorship right where Roy Dutton left off. It was interesting that he married one of his callers."

"They had an interesting beginning," Rebecca replied. "I've been impressed with what Beth has done with her life. She came to Rocky Bluff as an unwed teenage mother and was able to finish high school and a secretarial course at the college. When she got a job at the school she was a tremendous help to me in the library."

"She went through a lot when her son was kidnapped. I never thought she'd see him again, but her prayers paid off."

"Even when he was gone she was disciplined enough to

27

focus her attention on her job. Everyone admired her for that."

"Dan and Beth would be the kind of people I would like caring for my home if I were to be gone for an extended period of time." Andy paused for a few moments before continuing. "The reason why I stopped over is to find out if you've noticed Dick Reed around the house."

Rebecca looked puzzled. "I haven't seen him since the day after the funeral. Dick and Anita's parents took the girls to Pat's basement to go through the clothes and toys donated to them. Dick said he was going to stay at the motel."

"I know," Andy replied. "I stopped by the motel a couple days ago to ask him more questions and the manager said he left town and he didn't know where he was."

"That's strange. Does anyone know where he went?"

The fire chief wrinkled his forehead. "Not as far as I can discover. I called Anita's parents in Spokane and they were surprised that he was gone."

"Have they found the cause of the fire yet?"

"Not yet. But it looks like it started in the hallway near a space heater. That's why I wanted to talk to him."

"You aren't suspecting foul play are you?"

"At this point we're not ruling anything out. I need to know the condition and history of the space heater."

"I'm curious how all of this is going to develop. I hope that I'll be able to keep in touch with people in Rocky Bluff and not miss out on any of the news."

"I'll try to keep you updated," Andy assured her. "After all, if this does go to court you'll be one of the star witnesses."

"I won't be of much help half a world away, but I'll make a written statement of what I know."

"That's all that's necessary," Andy assured her. He glanced at his watch. "It's getting late. I promised the crew I'd be back at the fire hall by four and it's nearly five till. I hope I'll have a chance to see you before you leave."

Blood rushed to Rebecca face. "I'd like that. I'm leaving on the seven o'clock flight to Billings and then on to Seattle."

"How about a farewell dinner for two at the Steak House Saturday night?"

"Sounds good to me," Rebecca replied with a smile. "This time I hope I'm a little more alert than the last time we were there."

Andy grinned as he stood to leave. "Even in our most exhausted state we had a good time together, so Saturday has got to be exciting."

The days passed quickly as Rebecca sorted and packed her personal belongings. What to take and what to store was a constant dilemma. During her busy moments she looked forward to a relaxing evening with Andy at the Steak House. She wanted to savor every moment she had with her friends in Rocky Bluff, knowing that it probably would be two years before she would see them again.

"Rebecca, I really envy you getting to spend a couple weeks in Hawaii," Andy said as he finished his baked Alaska that Saturday evening. "My favorite aunt lives there and when I was a boy we'd go visit her every couple years."

"What fond memories," Rebecca smiled. "What was she doing on the islands? Did she have an outside job?"

"My uncle was stationed at Scofield Barracks during World War II. After the war was over he got a civilian job at the naval shipyard and she opened a dress shop in downtown Honolulu," Andy explained. "He died fifteen years ago. Aunt Lucille sold her store five years later and has spent the last few years basking in the sun."

Rebecca's eyes sparkled with interest. "When was the last time you got to see her?"

"I went over for Uncle Gene's funeral and I haven't been back since. They never had children of their own so they kind of adopted me, especially after my folks died while I was in college. Do you think you might have time to call her while you're there? I'm sure she'd love to hear from someone from Rocky Bluff. I've told her so much about Montana and this town."

"I'd love to," Rebecca replied with a smile. "Just write down her phone number and I'll do my best. Since I'm not traveling with anyone it will be good to talk with someone I have something in common with."

Andy took a notepad from his pocket along with his address book. He hurriedly copied the ten digits on a scrap of paper and handed it to Rebecca. She folded it and placed it in the outer flap of her purse. In the process she glanced at her watch. "It's been a delightful evening," she said, "but I'm afraid all good things have to come to an end. I still have a lot more packing to get done before I can go to bed tonight."

Sadness enveloped Rebecca as Andy drove her home. She had spent many years in Rocky Bluff without any serious interest in male companionship, but on the eve of her departure Andy had ignited a warmth in her that she thought had long since been extinguished.

⛧

That Sunday afternoon Rebecca stopped at the Dutton residence. "Edith, I wanted to be sure and see Roy before I left town. Would you like to ride to the care center with me?"

"Thanks for the offer," Edith replied. "Usually Dan Blair gives me a ride, but he had to work."

As Rebecca turned onto Main Street she smiled at her friend beside her. "I appreciate you letting me store my car in your garage while I'm gone. I was at a loss as to what to do with it since it's too new to sell."

"I'm glad I could help," Edith assured her. "The garage has been empty ever since Roy had his stroke and we gave his car to our grandson Jay."

"I've seen it parked in the student parking lot," Rebecca said. "Jay's a responsible young man and is taking good care of it. That car seems to be his pride and joy."

Rebecca was not prepared for the change in Roy's condition since she had last seen him a couple months before. He had lost over thirty pounds and his hair hung limp and lifeless. He forced a smile as the two women entered his room.

Rebecca approached his recliner and took his hand. "Hello, Roy," she greeted. "How are you today?"

"F . . . f . . . fine," he whispered.

"I'm glad to hear that," Rebecca replied with a forced smile. "I'm leaving for Guam Monday and wanted to come and say good-bye. I'm going to miss you."

Roy tried to speak, but Rebecca could not understand his words. She looked at Edith.

"He's trying to say, 'Please write,'" Edith explained.

"I'll try to write often," Rebecca assured him as she held his hand. "I'm going to take a two week vacation in Hawaii on my way over so I'll send you some picture postcards from there."

Rebecca took a chair in the corner while Edith shared the family news with her husband, read a few articles of interest from the *Rocky Bluff Herald* and a couple of chapters from his Bible.

A few minutes later while they walked down the corridor

toward the nurses' station Rebecca made sure she didn't look Edith's way. Tears filled her eyes. *Will this be the last time I'll get to see Roy?* she mused as a wave of melancholy enveloped her.

Just as planned, at seven o'clock that evening the Blairs rang Rebecca's doorbell. "Welcome to your new home," Rebecca greeted. "Do come in and I'll show you around."

Dan, Beth, and four-year-old Jeffey followed Rebecca into her spacious living room.

"It's beautiful," Beth gasped. "You have excellent tastes in decorating."

"Thanks," Rebecca smiled. "I hope you'll be as happy in this house as I've been."

"I'm sure we will be," Beth replied. "I feel honored that you asked us to care for it while you're gone."

Rebecca patted Beth on the shoulder. "After working with you for the last few months there's no one else I'd rather have live here."

"I promise I'll take good care of your dog," Jeffey said as he knelt to pet the Pekingese at his feet. "I've never had a dog of my own. This'll be fun."

"Her name is Shushu. Come and I'll show you where his food is kept," Rebecca said as she motioned for them to follow her to the back porch.

While Jeffey played with the Shushu, Rebecca showed Dan and Beth where the fuse box was, the water and gas shut-off valves, along with the lawn mower and other outdoor tools. Beth felt overwhelmed with the responsibility of such a large home to care for, but Dan took it in stride and rose to the challenge.

After discussing every possible problem that might arise, Rebecca handed a set of house keys to Dan. "I wish I were able to give you a forwarding address and telephone number, but I won't know until I get there. I'll call you long distance as soon as I have that information. Good luck."

Beth hugged her former supervisor and bade her farewell. She had depended on Rebecca a great deal during Jeffey's kidnapping the previous fall and it was hard to say good-bye. Yet, the excitement of her new life with Dan could not be dampened.

❧

The warm tropical breeze rushed through Rebecca's hair as she stepped from the Honolulu Airport. The van to the Royal Hawaiian Hotel waited at the curbside. A flood of memories enveloped her as she directed the Red Cap where to unload her luggage and then handed him a tip. This was a part of her life that she rarely shared with her friends from Rocky Bluff.

As the van weaved in and out of the traffic everything seemed so different, and yet Rebecca felt so connected to the island. It had been more than twenty-five years since she was last there but now it seemed like only yesterday. She remembered standing at Eric's gravesite at the Pacific War Memorial Cemetery in the Punchbowl. He had been cited for bravery after being killed trying to save his platoon during the Tet Offensive of the Vietnam War. *I wonder what our lives together would have been if he would have returned? Would we still be teaching somewhere in Iowa? Would we have had a family?* Rebecca wondered.

Rebecca's attention was shaken back to reality as the van swerved to avoid hitting a group of pedestrians illegally crossing the street. *I have to enjoy today,* she scolded herself, *instead of dwelling on what might have been. I want to enjoy the island like all the other vacationers and not play the grieving widow of bygone days.*

Just as she promised herself, Rebecca spent the next three

days playing tourist. She lounged on the beach, she walked the Ala Moana Mall, she visited the U.S.S. Arizona Memorial, yet amid all the glitter and excitement of Hawaii a nagging emptiness hung over her. She tried writing postcards to her friends in Rocky Bluff—Edith Dutton, Beth Blair, Andy Hatfield, Pat Crouse, Teresa Lennon. Yet even the memory of her favorite people could not remove loneliness.

The walls of the Rocky Bluff High School Library had always served as her refuge and a cushion against pain. This fall someone new would be in her place and Beth Blair would be that person's loyal assistant. *Am I strong enough to face another culture alone for two years?* Rebecca worried. *I've always prided myself on my independence and self-reliance, so why should I be so fearful about being alone?*

Rebecca's attention returned to the tropical surroundings. *This is silly,* she scolded herself as she watched the native dancers perform at the luau on the beach. *Tomorrow I'm going to take the city bus to the Punchbowl. I know he's no longer there, but maybe by being at his grave this restlessness will disappear and I'll be able to face the future unencumbered by memories.*

Just as she had planned, the next day Rebecca hiked a mile uphill from the last bus stop to the cemetery. The view over the city was awe inspiring. Yet, something was missing. The beauty and dignity of this honored cemetery had been transformed into a park atmosphere. Tour buses containing visitors from seemingly every county in the world converged on what she considered sacred ground. *These are our country's honored dead,* she thought. *The foreigners have no concept what this place means to us. Before I leave Hawaii I must register my protest of turn-*

ing a national memorial into a tourist attraction.

Rebecca walked directly to her husband's gravesite. Every blade of grass was well manicured. She knelt beside the marker expecting a flood of ancient grief to overwhelm her; instead a calm peace settled over her. Eric had been in the loving hands of God for more than a quarter of a century, yet she had not released his memory and could not develop a deep friendship with any other man.

As the fresh mowed grass tickled her knees, she felt as if she heard him say, "Rebecca, I loved you dearly during the brief years we had together. Don't hide your life surrounded by books; learn to love again. Life is too short to waste a single moment."

Joy swelled up from within as she rose to her feet. That inner emptiness that had long imprisoned her faded. During the downhill walk to the bus stop she felt as if she were gliding on a cloud.

The next morning at breakfast the date on the morning newspaper nearly jumped off the page. *My vacation is nearly over and I haven't called Andy's aunt like I promised him.*

After finishing her breakfast of tropical fruit, Rebecca hurried back to her room. She thumbed through her purse until she found the wrinkled paper containing Lucille Hatfield's telephone number.

Rebecca dialed the number and waited. "Hello. Lucille Hatfield residence," a familiar male voice answered.

Rebecca hesitated. "Andy is that you?"

"Rebecca, I was hoping you'd call. I wanted to call you but I had no idea where you were staying."

"What are you doing in Honolulu?"

"Two days after you left I received a call that Aunt Lucille had passed away. Since I'm the next of kin, I caught the next flight out of Rocky Bluff so I could be here to make the final arrangements."

Rebecca sank onto her hotel bed. "I'm sorry to hear that. I know she'd been extra special to you throughout the years."

"That she was," Andy confessed. "It was very hard for me to leave the cemetery yesterday. I'm trying to get all the loose ends tied together today so I can leave first thing in the morning. It's vacation time and I can't leave. The fire department is shorthanded."

"Lucille was fortunate to have a nephew as considerate as you," Rebecca reminded him as she pictured his concerned eyes and broad shoulders.

"This is my last night on the island and I'd love to spend it with you," Andy replied. "Where would you suggest?"

"They're serving dinner on the hotel patio here at the Royal Hawaiian this evening. They're bringing in native dancers and we could dine by the beach and watch the sun go down."

"That sounds perfect," Andy replied as his sense of mourning for his favorite aunt lifted. "I have some errands to run and then I'll meet you at six-thirty."

The musicians strummed their ukuleles while Andy and Rebecca sipped their fruit drinks on the patio of the Royal Hawaiian. The palm trees rustled gently in the background. Tonight was the first time in more than twenty-five years that Rebecca had felt the concerned friendship of a man. They laughed and talked and shared many of their hopes and dreams of the future. There was never a mention of the tragedy that had occurred next door to her which brought them together. The sparkle in her eyes was like a woman of eighteen facing the world of love for the first time. Was it possible for a relationship to develop when they were eighteen thousand miles apart and would not see each other for two years?

four

"Hafa adai," the clerk at the rent-a-car booth in the Won Pat International Airport greeted. "May I help you?"

"I'd like to rent an economy car for a week," Rebecca said as she parked her luggage cart in front of the counter.

"We have a two-door Mazda available," the bronzed-skinned woman responded briskly as she reached in the file beside her. "If you're interested, please fill out the following forms."

Rebecca surveyed the questionnaire and shook her head with frustration. "What do I put down for an address? I just got off the plane and haven't had time to go apartment hunting."

"Just write in the name of the hotel where you'll be staying. On Guam, we know the car won't be going far," the clerk chuckled.

"I haven't checked into a hotel yet," Rebecca sighed. "Do you have any suggestions?"

"I suggest the Pacific Star, it's one of the nicest on Guam. Would you like a map of the island?"

"I'd appreciate that," Rebecca replied as she continued filling in the blanks. "I'll treat myself to a nice room tonight and go apartment hunting tomorrow."

The clerk entered the data into the computer and handed her a set of keys. "You'll find your car parked in space A-seventeen."

"Thanks for your help," Rebecca replied as she adjusted the luggage on her cart. The rusted wheels balked as she

headed toward the automatic door. She looked for Red
Cap assistance, but none was available. People from all
nationalities filled the lobby. Everyone seemed oblivious
of her presence. *I have to learn to be totally self-suffi-
cient,* Rebecca reminded herself. *I've been spoiled by
having spent most of my adult life in Rocky Bluff. If I
were struggling with this load there I'd have a host of
people helping me.*

ॡ

The heavy tropical air smothered Rebecca as she stepped
from the airport in Tamuning, Guam. Perspiration began
running down her forehead. She was used to the tempera-
tures occasionally reaching the high nineties in Montana
during July and August, but those couldn't compare with
the oppressive eighty-eight humid degrees of island life.
She piled her luggage in the trunk of the rental car, returned the cart to the terminal, and started the engine of
her rented Mazda. *Ahh, air conditioning at last.*

Rebecca was scarcely able to absorb the extreme con-
trasts in her surroundings. She expected Guam to be just
like Hawaii, only smaller, but the differences shocked her.
While driving the few miles to the Pacific Star she mar-
veled at the international cosmopolitanism side-by-side with
tin shacks. Chickens ran loose through the yards. Small
children played barefoot while older ones gathered under
the palm trees with soft drinks in their hands. Life seemed
as if it were right out of *National Geographic.* She surveyed the young people she passed with wonderment.
Could they be some of my future students? she mused.
*Will I be able to relate to them and help them learn to use
a library? Did I do the right thing to come so far by
myself?*

Rebecca stopped her rented Mazda at a corner gas station and studied her newly-acquired map. After surveying her surroundings and the traffic patterns, she started the car. At the next corner she turned west toward Tumon Bay. She gasped as she saw the marble-colored hotel rising above the bright blue shoreline. This was more beautiful than anything she had seen in Hawaii. *The rental agency clerk was right,* she mentally gasped. *This one night of luxury will be well worth the investment.*

Within minutes Rebecca had checked into the Pacific Star and was helped to her room on the fourth floor. After tipping the bellboy she turned to the window and pulled open the drapes. The sky was ablaze with reds and oranges as it settled upon the watery horizon. Instead of being overwhelmed by the beauty so different from the majestic mountains of Montana, tears filled Rebecca's eyes. *I've never felt this alone since I got word of Eric's death more than twenty-five years ago. Instead of the ocean welcoming me, it feels like a chasm separating me from my loved ones in Rocky Bluff, Montana.*

Rebecca opened the drawer of the dresser and took out the hotel stationery. She flopped across the bed. *I haven't written a letter for years. Picking up the telephone is too easy, but I need to share the mixed emotions welling within me.*

> *Dear Edith,*
>   *After a five-hour nonstop flight from Hawaii I finally arrived in Guam. It's so different from what I expected. I thought it would be a miniature Hawaii, but it's like I am in a foreign country instead of a U.S. territory.*
>   *Last night I was dining under a palm tree*

on the patio of the Royal Hawaiian Hotel on Waikiki beach with Andy Hatfield. I was shocked when I called his aunt and Andy answered the phone himself. His beloved aunt had passed away suddenly. I was glad I could be there during that difficult time for him. I never thought I'd ever again have a deep relationship with another man, but since the Reeds' fire I'm catching myself thinking more and more about Andy. The few hours we've had together have meant so much to me.

As I look across the Philippine Sea from my hotel room memories of home envelop me. I remember the glow that grew within you as your relationship with Roy deepened. At your retirement party from the high school I knew you'd continue to have a productive life, but little did I imagine that love could happen to someone over sixty. Now that I'm nearing that age myself, I'm wondering if the same thing could happen to me. However, I won't be back to Rocky Bluff for nearly two years so there's no way love can grow across the distant sea.

I suppose I'd better close now and get some sleep. Jet lag is beginning to set in. It will probably be several days before my internal clock adjusts to crossing the international dateline. The next few days are going to be extremely busy. I have to stop by Guam Christian Academy and let them know I'm on the island. I hope I can find an

*apartment right away. (I can't afford to stay
in this luxury for long.) I'll also need to buy
a car right away. Renting one can certainly
add up in a hurry.*

*I'll let you know my permanent address
just as soon as I find an apartment. Say
hello to Beth and Dan for me, and give a
special greeting to Andy.*

May God continue to bless you and Roy,
Rebecca

ು

The day after Chief Hatfield returned from Hawaii, Captain Philip Mooney walked into his office at the fire station. "Andy, it's good to have you back. How was your trip?"

"I wish I could say it was a delightful vacation of lying on the beach at Waikiki, but it was extremely difficult saying my final farewell to Aunt Lucille. The only enjoyable thing about the entire week was that I met up with Rebecca Sutherland. Just having a sympathetic ear of someone from Rocky Bluff meant so much to me. I just hope and pray things go well for her on Guam. From some of the stories I've heard about Guam, I'm concerned about her being over there by herself."

"I'm sure she'll be all right," Phil tried to assure him. "We both saw how good she was in crisis management the night of the Reeds' fire."

"She was brilliant and rose to the occasion," Andy agreed. Suddenly his eyes became serious. "Have there been any new developments in the case while I was gone?"

A scowl spread across Phil's face. "We haven't been able to figure out the exact cause of the fire. We're sure it started around a space heater in the hallway in front of the master bedroom, but it appeared to be a new heater so it doesn't make sense." Phil shook his head with despair. "Dick Reed has left town and no one seems to know where he went. . .not even his in-laws. Add to that, he took out a million dollar life insurance policy on his wife just three months ago. They're holding payment until we complete our investigation."

Andy stroked his chin. "Sounds pretty suspicious. Do you think it's time we call in Marty Sanchez again? He did wonders in finding the cause of the Harkness Hardware Store fire a few years ago."

Phil stroked his chin. "Speaking of Harkness Hardware, I wonder if the Reeds bought the space heater there. It looks fairly new. I think I'll stop by there later this afternoon and see if Bob has any records on it."

"Sounds like a good possibility," Andy replied. "We don't have many clues to go on. Maybe Marty will unearth the truth."

"We need all the help we can get. I'll give the state crime lab a call in the morning," Phil replied. "Hopefully they can get their top arson investigator here before the end of the week."

"If there's proof of arson we don't want to let Dick get too far away from us." Andy hesitated. "Three months ago Dick Reed seemed like such a respectable family man and now all sorts of weird things are surfacing."

ஃ

"Dan, I certainly appreciate you giving me a ride to the nursing home each afternoon. I don't know how Roy or I can ever repay you," Edith said as they approached the Rocky Bluff Care Center.

"You and Roy have meant so much to Beth and me that even if we lived until we were a hundred we could never repay you for what you've done for us." Dan's mind drifted back through the years. "Roy was the one responsible for getting me involved in the crisis center and you were always there for Beth when she first came to town as a frightened single mother. Even little Jeffey thinks you're the greatest."

Edith smiled. "We've certainly been through a lot together, haven't we?"

Dan reached across the seat and patted Edith's hand. "You've been there for us during both the good times and the bad. You've literally become our surrogate parents."

The pair rode in silence for several blocks before Edith spoke again. "I just got a letter from Rebecca. She says hello to you and Beth. She sounds awfully lonesome."

"Beth and I would like to write to her, but we don't have an address yet," Dan acknowledged. "I suppose we could write to her in care of the school where she's going to work. She's planning to check in there just as soon as she gets to Guam. I'm sure she'd like to know how Shushu is doing."

Dan stopped the car in the handicapped parking spot in front of the nursing home so Edith would not have to strain herself with a long walk. "I'll see you in a couple hours," he said as his older friend opened the passenger door. "I have a few errands to run for the crisis center this afternoon."

As Edith stopped at the nurses' station to check on Roy's condition, Liz Chapman, the activities director approached. "Edith, how good to see you."

Edith beamed as she took the young woman's hand. "Hello, Liz. You're looking extremely vibrant today. Things must be going well for you."

"I've never found a job as rewarding as this one. I only wish I had more time to arrange for local talent to perform at our afternoon get-togethers."

"Rocky Bluff has a lot of untapped talent," Edith replied. "I'm amazed every time I attend a school or community activity."

Liz nodded as she remembered the high school music concert the previous week. "Would you be willing to run interference for me? I'd like to schedule performances every Monday, Wednesday, and Friday, and in-house games on Tuesday and field trips on Thursday."

"I'd be honored. In fact, I know of several groups who would be happy to play here."

"Thanks a heap. It'll mean so much to the residents," Liz replied.

"Roy looks forward to your talent days and is always asking when the next one is going to be. Making contacts is the least I can do to help. I'll get on the phone just as soon as I get home," Edith promised.

Edith said good-bye to Liz and then slipped into Roy's room. Seeing his bride of less than five years, Roy sat up in his recliner and beamed. "H. . . H. . . Hi. . .h. . .h. . . hon. . . n. . . ney."

Edith leaned over and kissed him on the lips. "Hello. How are you doing?"

Roy nodded affirmatively as Edith pulled a chair close to his. "I brought the mail along to read. I got a letter from Rebecca Sutherland in Guam. Would you like to have me read it to you?"

Roy again nodded his head. His eyes portrayed intense interest as Edith read the letter. "N. . . N. . . nice," he muttered as she finished reading and folded the letter.

Edith then read the main articles in the *Herald* to him. Before she was finished with the sports page, Roy was asleep. Edith took her knitting from her bag and began working on a new lap robe for him. She treasured every moment she had with her husband, even those when he was sleeping.

It didn't seem long before Dan was there to give her a ride home. "Hi," he greeted as he stepped into the room. "I was looking forward to visiting with Roy a few minutes before we left, but I see he's sleeping."

"No problem," Edith replied. "The nurses have encouraged me to awaken him when he has company. They feel he can sleep anytime and the mental stimulation of a familiar face will help keep his mind in touch with the outside world."

Edith gently shook her husband's shoulder. "Roy, you have company."

Roy sleepily opened his eyes. A broad grin spread across his face. "D. . . D. . . Dan," he stuttered.

Dan shook his older friend's hand and then began sharing some of the events of the crisis center. Roy listened with great interest. He started the Rocky Bluff Crisis Center soon after he retired from his social services career. Turning the center over to Dan was one of the hardest things he had ever done. Roy's eyes sparkled with each new event and he nodded with approval with each change. Although Roy's speech was limited his eyes still communicated his inner vitality and strength.

ॐ

Ten days after arriving in Guam, Rebecca walked into the principal's office at Guam Christian Academy. The room was not air-conditioned, but the louvres were open and a tropical breeze greeted her.

"Mr. Diaz, I'd like to thank you for helping me get settled here in Guam. I found a nice one-bedroom furnished apartment in Dededo. It's a little further than I'd like to drive, but this was the best I looked at."

"I'm glad I could help," David Diaz said as he motioned for her to sit down in the chair beside his desk. "How is the Toyota working out for you?"

Rebecca smiled. "Great. I understand it belonged to the social studies teacher."

"It's kind of a custom here," Mr. Diaz smiled. "When people return to the mainland, they need their car until they step onto the plane and they don't have time to find a buyer. When the new teachers arrive late in the summer the first thing they need is a car. We like to take the cars from the departing teachers and make them available to the incoming ones."

"It's a great system. It saved me a lot of problems."

"There's enough difficulties just getting here and settled. We like to make it as easy as possible. When we hire teachers from the mainland we look for those with good problem-solving abilities," Mr. Diaz explained. "You came highly recommended. Too many statesiders think coming to Guam will be like moving to another state. When they find they can't cope with the cultural differences, they're on the plane home before their first Christmas here."

"That's too bad," Rebecca replied, "but I can seen how that can happen." Her mind drifted back to the petite blond she had met the day before. "A young teacher just moved into the apartment across the hall. She returned from shopping yesterday nearly in tears. Someone had referred to her as a 'haole.' She hadn't heard the term before, but it was said with such disdain she knew she was being put down.

Mr. Diaz nodded his head knowingly, his bronze face reflecting a depth of understanding. "I'm sorry to say, that is a common occurrence here. The word 'haole' is

Hawaiian not Chammoro. It means 'boss.' During plantation days in Hawaii, the bigger plantations imported laborers from Japan, Korea, China, and the Philippines, and overseers from the U.S. mainland, Scotland, and Portugal. The overseers were called 'haole.' Since the bosses were all white, the word was soon corrupted and came to mean white. Unfortunately, today it has taken on a derogatory connotation and some of our people who should know better have adopted it as their own. The present interracial climate here is becoming more and more volatile. Is this your first experience as a minority?"

"I'll admit I've been pretty sheltered from racial slurs in Rocky Bluff. But being a minority here will give me a better understanding of what our Native Americans go through in Montana," Rebecca said. She hesitated as she grasped the enormity of the challenge of helping a people who might resent those of her homeland. "I'll do my best to provide the best school library possible and try to avoid any political or racial confrontations," Rebecca assured her new principal, trying hard to hide her trepidations.

"We're extremely fortunate to have you on our staff," Mr. Diaz replied. He then paused and pulled open his left-hand drawer. "By the way, several letters for you have already arrived. You must be a pretty popular person back in Montana."

Rebecca blushed as he handed her a stack of letters. "I'm sorry for the inconvenience. I had to give the school as my address until I found an apartment."

"No problem. Most of our new teachers do the same thing. In fact, we're still getting letters for teachers who left the island several years ago."

Principal Diaz handed Rebecca several brochures about the culture and life on Guam. "These might help you understand the local customs and people."

Rebecca thanked him and walked into the bright Guam sunshine. On the way to her car she thumbed through the pile of envelopes in her hand. *Hmmm. . . a letter from Beth Blair, one from Edith, one from Pat Crouse, another from Teresa Lennon.* Rebecca's eyes froze, her heart raced. The return address on the next envelope read: "Andrew Hatfield, 708 Maple St., Rocky Bluff, Montana." *Does Andy care enough about me to carry on a relationship from such a distance? Or. . . Maybe there's been new developments in the investigation of the Reeds' fire.*

five

Rebecca hurriedly unlocked the car door and rolled down the windows. She could not wait to drive across the island to her apartment before reading her mail. Her hand trembled and her palms became sweaty in the tropical heat as she tore open the letter from Andy.

> *Dear Rebecca,*
>
> *It was extremely fortunate that we were able to spend time together in Hawaii. I felt the loss of Aunt Lucille more intensely than ever I thought I would. Having you there did more than fill the void of Aunt Lucille; for the first time I felt what the Bible must mean when it says, "it's not good for man to be alone". All my life I've devoted myself to my career, but now I'm discovering another dimension to my life that I never thought existed . . .a need to share the joys and disappointments of everyday life with someone. Rebecca, when I was feeling low in Hawaii you were the one who helped lift me from despair. I'm looking forward to the day you return to Rocky Bluff for good.*
>
> *Incidentally, to bring you up to date on the happenings of Rocky Bluff, Dick Reed has left town and no one knows where he is. The fire is still under investigation and it's*

*looking more and more suspicious with each
passing day. Philip Mooney is going to call
the crime lab in Missoula to send out their
best arson investigator. Marty Sanchez did a
tremendous job at getting to the source of the
fire at Harkness Hardware Store a few years
ago so hopefully he'll be able to solve this
one as well. I'll keep you posted as to the
developments.*

  *Do be careful while you're overseas.
Guam is not nearly as safe as Rocky Bluff.*

                              God's blessings,
                                        Andy

The tropical breeze could not melt the oppressive heat
within Rebecca's Toyota. She started the engine, rolled up
the windows and turned on the air conditioner. The cool
air refreshed her perspiring body. She turned onto the highway and headed toward Dededo. The other letters could
wait. Her mind was in a spin. In less than a week school
would be starting and she had so much to learn. Life on
Guam was so different from life in Rocky Bluff. The easy-
going, relaxed atmosphere was foreign to the work ethic
displayed in a cold climate. The emphasis on education
had always been vital to rural Montana while education
on Guam was just beginning to experience its awakening.
*Maybe I should enroll in the class "Education and Cul-
ture on Guam" that's being offered at the University of
Guam this fall,* Rebecca mused as she parked her car in
front of her apartment building. She took the letters from
the dash of her car and hurried inside. *I'm sure glad friends
in Rocky Bluff haven't forgotten me,* she sighed. *I feel like
a fish out of water walking on the beaches under the palm*

trees watching people relaxing in the sun.

Rebecca took a soft drink from the refrigerator and sunk into the cushion of her wicker sofa. She tore open Edith's letter hoping to find words of encouragement. She was not disappointed. Her eyes moistened as she read Edith's prompting to rely more on Christ during her lonesome moments than she ever had in her life.

"Situations that you normally would have discussed with a friend here in Rocky Bluff," Edith wrote, "you'll now have to talk to the Lord instead. Your friends may have given you some misguided advice throughout the years, but God will never lead you astray."

Rebecca paused. *Edith is right as usual. I have become too dependent on my friends instead of leaning totally on God. That's why I'm feeling so alone.*

☙

"Grandma, what would you think if I joined the air force after I graduate instead of going to college?" Jay Harkness asked as he sat across the kitchen table from his beloved grandmother.

Edith surveyed her handsome, athletic grandson. The resemblance to his father, Bob, at that age was remarkable. "Each person has to decide what's best for them," she replied. "What to do after high school is one of the biggest decisions you'll ever have to make."

"So I'm finding out," Jay replied. "I know you and Dad have assumed I'd go to the University of Montana and get a degree in business so I could come back and run the hardware store."

Edith looked stunned. "I'm sorry if I ever gave you that impression. More than anything I want you to be happy. Your grandfather and I enjoyed our life together running the store, but that doesn't mean everyone else would."

"Dad has always been wrapped up in the store and never seemed to have time to spend with us when we were little," Jay lamented. "Only once did we take an extended family vacation. That was when we went to California to see Great Aunt Phyllis when Uncle John died."

"That's true," Edith agreed. "As a store owner long vacations are often out, but you took many short vacations to Yellowstone Park, Glacier Park, and Flathead Lake. People drive clear across the country to see what we have right at our back door."

Jay blushed. "I don't want to seem ungrateful, but I guess I'm suffering from wanderlust. I want to travel and see the world. I figure the best way to do that is join the military. I can still work on a college degree while I'm in the service."

"You don't have to convince me of that," Edith replied. "Both Roy and your grandfather served in the second world war. They had pretty horrible stories to tell, but they both said the same thing. . .it gave them a better appreciation of different cultures and the value of human life."

"Dad doesn't see any future in military service. He seems to think the military is only for those who wouldn't be able to make it in college."

Edith paused. Her mind raced back through the years of political and social change she had seen in her lifetime. "Regardless of the isolation we sometimes feel in Montana, world events do shape individual attitudes and perceptions," she explained. "Your dad grew up in the Vietnam era. He served time in the army, but fortunately the war was over before he had to go overseas. Several of his friends from basic training were killed in the war and he never could find a reason for their death. Since then he's totally blocked out the necessity for a national defense system."

Jay nodded. "That explains his refusal. Every time we go to Great Falls I've always wanted to stop and visit Malmstrom Air Force Base, but he's always had a reason not to. It's like a curtain is drawn around him."

Seriousness entered Edith's soft voice. "Jay, you'll have to make your decision with your own life goals and objectives in mind. Your father loves you, he may object at first, but in the end he'll be the strongest ally you'll ever have."

"Dad has never let me down yet," Jay replied. "Right now I just want to get outside of Rocky Bluff and see the world." The young man shrugged his shoulders. "Maybe someday I'll want to move back to Rocky Bluff, but not for a long while. I envy Mrs. Sutherland getting to go to Guam to work for a couple years. I can just picture her lying under a palm tree drinking guava juice."

"Life in a distant land isn't always as glamorous as it may seem," Edith chuckled. "There's also the inconvenience of not having all the amenities of home. There's the loneliness of not being accepted into another culture. Judging from Rebecca's letters that seems to be her biggest concern at this time. It takes an extremely mature personality to do what she has done and I'm certain that Guam Christian Academy will profit greatly from her expertise."

The conversation shifted to the start of football season. Ever since Edith was the high school home economics teacher, she had always enjoyed following Rocky Bluff High School athletic games. Now that her grandson played both on the football and basketball teams she enjoyed them even more. Before each game Jay always looked into the stands to locate his family.

A note of sadness enveloped Jay. This year Roy would not be at his grandmother's side. A series of strokes had made it impossible for him to leave the nursing home. "Grandma, would you like to ride to Great Falls with me Saturday? I'd like to visit the base there before I talk to the recruiter. I want to make sure this is the right decision without any outside pressure or fantastic offers."

"I'd love to," Edith replied. "I'll treat you to the best restaurant in town while we're there."

༄

Captain Philip Mooney reached for the phone in the Rocky Bluff Police Station and dialed the number of the state crime lab in Missoula.

"State Crime Lab. How may I direct your call?"

"Director Bruce Devlin, please."

Phil listened as he heard several clicks on the line. Then a friendly voice said, "Director's Office. May I help you?"

"This is Captain Mooney of the Rocky Bluff Police Department. Is Bruce Devlin available?"

"He's on another line. Would you care to hold?"

"Sure," Phil said as soft music began playing in the background. He reached for some paperwork on his desk to occupy his time while he waited.

Within minutes a voice came over the phone. "Hello, Phil. How's things in Rocky Bluff? Are you staying above the crime wave?"

"Speeding tickets are my specialty," Phil chuckled as he recognized the voice of the head of the crime lab. "However, this time I'm stymied by a possible arson case."

"Did you have another hardware store burn down?"

"Worse than that," Phil replied. "This time it was a house fire. The mother and two children died in the blaze. It's a strange situation and now the husband has left town and we don't know where he is."

Bruce Devlin's voice became somber. "Sounds pretty

serious. With the husband having left town a lot of the evidence probably left with him. I'll send Marty Sanchez over first thing in the morning."

"Our Fire Chief, Andrew Hatfield, will be glad to see him," Phil replied. "He's becoming extremely frustrated with the situation. He has strong suspicions but little evidence."

"That's Marty's specialty," Bruce replied. "Please have someone meet the ten-thirty Treasure State flight from Missoula tomorrow morning."

ə.

At ten o'clock the next morning Chief Hatfield and Captain Mooney drove to the airport outside of Rocky Bluff to meet Julio Raphael Martinez Sanchez. The eighteen passenger Treasure State commuter had become an invaluable link between Rocky Bluff and the rest of the world.

The pair peered toward the western sky until the small plane appeared. It rolled to a stop and the side door opened, releasing the steps. Marty was the first off the plane dressed in his customary Montana traveling garb of blue jeans, western shirt, and cowboy boots.

"Welcome back to Rocky Bluff," Captain Mooney greeted as he extended his hand. "I believe you met Fire Chief Hatfield during your last visit."

Marty nodded in greeting and shook both men's hands. "It's good to see you again. I only wish we could meet under better circumstances."

"After the investigation is over why don't you stick around and I'll treat you to dinner at Beefy's Steak House," Phil offered.

"Sounds good to me," Marty replied. "But first things first. Let's go over the evidence you have so far."

"Right now everything's locked in my office awaiting

your arrival," Andy explained. "Our prime piece of evidence is a space heater. We believe it started the fire. The thing that has me stumped is that it's a brand new heater. We checked with Bob Harkness at the hardware store. He went through all his back records and found that Dick Reed purchased the heater just a week before the fire. A new heater shouldn't have overheated."

On the way to the fire station Andy rehashed the events of the night of the fire. "The temperature dipped to a new record low for the month of June that night," he explained. "Around two in the morning Dick Reed awakened the next door neighbor and asked her to call the fire department. We found it extremely strange that he didn't try to get his family out first, but he maintains he was confused and frightened by the intensity of the flames. Also, he had taken out a million dollar life insurance policy on his wife just three months prior to the fire."

"I'd like to talk with that neighbor," Marty stated. "Maybe in the confusion Dick might have said something that would help the investigation."

Andy's eyes became distant. "I'm sorry, but that won't be possible. Rebecca Sutherland is now on Guam. I did interview her extensively before she left and you're welcome to use those notes and tapes."

Marty sighed. "That will help."

"I have her address and telephone number," Andy replied. "We could always give her a call. International calls have become nearly as easy as local ones."

"I'll make my investigation and then if there's any missing pieces I'll try to contact Mrs. Sutherland," Marty said. "A telephone call may not be necessary."

The three men hurried into the fire chief's office. The charred heater was on a table in the corner. Without saying a word, Marty picked up the heater and studied it from every possible angle. "Hmm. . . Interesting," he muttered as the two Rocky Bluff residents waited in silence. They had learned during his last investigation not to ask questions until Marty had completed his analysis.

Finally Marty looked up. "Andy, do you have a Phillips head screw driver handy?"

"It's in the back cupboard. Just a minute and I'll get the key to it," Andy replied as he reached into his desk drawer. He took the key and jiggled the lock until it opened and quickly located the desired tool.

Marty took the screw driver and removed the screws holding the casing to the rest of the heater. "Hmm. . .These are turning too easily. Has anyone taken this apart during the investigation?"

Andy's faced reddened. "I never thought to take it apart," he confessed.

"Most people don't," Marty replied as he removed the case. "It appears this heater has been tampered with."

Marty continued working in silence. "Hmm. . .Interesting," he mumbled. Finally he turned to his companions and pointed to the heater in his hand. "Do you notice anything missing?"

"No, I can't say that I do," Phil replied.

"The thermostat has been removed. When the heater was plugged in without a thermostat, the coils just got hotter and hotter until they ignited the closest flammable item. Had there been a thermostat in the heater, chances are there would have been no fire. The thermostat would have automatically turned off the heater when the temperature of the coils reached seventy-seven degrees. It also looks like the heater was lying on its side." Marty pointed to the inner coils. "Notice how one side of the coils are darker than the other. That is not a normal burn mark."

"Yes, I see it now," Andy said as he peered through his bifocals. "I should have thought of that myself."

"Has anything been moved in the house?" Marty asked. "I know its been two months since the fire."

"I went in there once with Dick to see if there was anything that could be salvaged, but it's been sealed ever since," Phil answered.

"Good. Let's go see the fire site," Marty responded as he moved toward the door before the others had a chance to respond.

Phil drove the police car down the familiar route to Rimrock Road. The charred house continued to send chills down his spine as memories of that tragic night two months before flashed through his mind. He waved at Dan Blair who was mowing the lawn next door as they stepped from the car. The contrast of the normal tasks of life and the horror next door momentarily paralyzed him.

Phil unlocked the door and Marty led the way into the house. He went straight to the hallway where the heater had been located. "Hmm. . . Interesting," Marty repeated. He got down on his hands and knees and felt the burnt carpeting. He picked up the charred remains of a child's receiving blanket. "Where was this located when you removed the heater?" he asked.

"It was underneath the heater," Andy replied. "With four small children in the house I assumed one of them had dropped it too close to the heater."

"A child would drop a blanket on top of a heater, not under it." Marty's eyes sparkled. "So. . .o. . .o," he stated as his voice trailed out. "The person who started the fire removed the thermostat from the heater, laid it on its side on top of a highly flammable blanket. The blanket ignited the carpet, which is very cheap and gives off noxious fumes when it burns. It's a miracle that the mother was able to get two of the children out of the house before the fumes overcame her."

"That's all I need to know," Phil stated, his eyes ablaze. "I'll prepare a report immediately for our county attorney, so that he can get the ball rolling for an arrest warrant. We can charge Dick Reed with three counts of homicide. We'll put that sleaze ball away for good."

six

Three hundred students and faculty gathered in the Guam Christian Academy gymnasium for the Opening Assembly of the new school year. Rebecca watched as the students filed in, giggling and laughing, glad to be back together after summer break. *There's little difference between these kids and those in Rocky Bluff except their skin is darker and their hair is shiny black,* Rebecca observed. *It looks like only ten percent of the student body are Anglos, or Haoles as they call us.*

"Hello," a voice from beside her greeted. "I take it you're the new librarian. I'm Mitzi Quinata, head of the English Department."

Rebecca turned and smiled. "Hi. I'm Rebecca Sutherland. It's nice meeting you."

"It's good having you at GCA. I've been pushing for two years to get a full-time librarian," Mitzi replied. "Without a good library it's nearly impossible to teach English properly. You have your work cut out for you."

Rebecca laughed. "To be honest I was a little overwhelmed when the principal first showed me the library. Boxes of books are stacked everywhere. A computer in the corner is still in boxes and the software is beside it. Within a short time I have to turn those boxes into an organized library."

"From what I've heard of your credentials I'm sure you'll do a great job," Mitzi replied. "If there's anything I can do to help, please let me know. When you're ready to shelve

books I'll have my students help you. It'll be a good learning experience for them. Most of them have never heard of
the Dewey Decimal System."

"Thanks for the offer," Rebecca replied as the principal
moved to the podium.

"Welcome to a new and exciting year at GCA," the principal began. "Let us all rise and sing the national anthem
and the Guam Hymn."

A lump gathered in Rebecca's throat as the familiar
strains of the national anthem began. Home seemed so far
away, yet she was bound to this room full of strangers by
the stars and stripes on the far wall. As soon as the excitement of the "Star Spangled Banner" ended, a soft hush
filled the room. The students and teachers displayed a
deeper respect as they sang the Guam Hymn in their own
Chamorro language.

This feels like a strange contradiction, Rebecca mused.
*A moment ago I felt a part of these people. Now I feel like
a visitor in a foreign country.*

The crowd remained standing while the principal led them
in prayer for wisdom and guidance. He asked for a special
blessing for all the students, faculty, and support staff. After
the final amen everyone was seated as the principal surveyed his student body with pride.

"Hafa adai. Greetings to each one of you. We've made
a lot of changes since last year. As you may have noticed
there's a new paint job throughout the school. The new
wing housing the library and audiovisual center has been
completed and we've hired a full-time librarian." He paused
as he surveyed the section where the faculty was sitting.
Spotting Rebecca, he motioned for her to stand. "Please
make our new librarian, Rebecca Sutherland, feel welcome."

Loud cheers and applause filled the gymnasium. Rebecca smiled and waved to the student body.

"Mrs. Sutherland, would you like to come to the microphone and say a few words?" Mr. Diaz said as the gym became quieter.

Rebecca walked to the front. "I'd like to thank you all for your warm welcome. I'm looking forward to getting to know each of you individually and having a great year together. May God bless you all."

The crowd again burst into cheers as Rebecca returned to her seat. "They're an enthusiastic bunch," she whispered to Mitzi as she joined her colleague.

"That's a Guamanian welcome," the English teacher whispered back. "The Chamorros are an extremely warm and friendly people."

After the assembly Rebecca returned to her library full of boxes. *Where do I begin?* she mused as she scrutinized the room. *I suppose I should assemble the computer first and load the software. Then I can catalog the books as I take them out of the boxes.*

The rest of the day flew by and when it was time to go home, Mitzi stuck her head into the library. "No one's allowed to work late on the first day of school," she teased as she scanned the room. "It looks like you got a lot done today."

"I feel like it," Rebecca sighed. "I'm exhausted, but at least I'll be able to begin cataloging books tomorrow."

Rebecca locked the library door and the pair walked to the parking lot together, exchanging first day of school stories. It was comforting to Rebecca for a local teacher to take her under her wing and explain the similarities and differences of the two cultures. Mitzi had been educated at Portland State University and was well aware of the subtle adjustments in moving from the mainland to Guam.

As Rebecca parked her car at her apartment in Dededo, Ella Mae Jackson pulled in beside her.

"Hello," she greeted. "How was your first day of school?"

The trim blond locked her car and joined her new friend on the curb.

"Much different from I expected," she confessed in a soft southern drawl. "Guam's nothing like Abbeville, South Carolina."

Rebecca snickered. "It's a lot different from Rocky Bluff, Montana, too. Why don't you come to my apartment so we can compare tales of woe?"

"Thanks," Ella Mae smiled, trying to hide her frustrations of the day. "I've been busy with students all day and have scarcely had a chance to talk with any adult."

Rebecca unlocked her apartment door and motioned for Ella Mae to make herself comfortable on the wicker sofa while she went to the refrigerator for soft drinks.

"You're lucky," Ella Mae began as her hostess handed her a glass of cool refreshment. "You've had a lot of experience as a librarian and teacher before you came to Guam. This is my first year teaching and I have to get used to both teaching and a different culture."

Rebecca surveyed her young friend's wrinkled forehead.

"What school were you finally assigned to?"

"George Washington High School. They say it's one of roughest ones on the island."

"Did you get a chance to meet any of the other faculty today?" Rebecca queried.

A faint smile began to spread across Ella Mae's face. "The head of the R.O.T.C. program stopped by my room during his lunch break to welcome me," she replied softly. "His name is Major Lee. I watched him work with the kids on the track trying to teach them to march. I thought he was terribly harsh and strict with them, but when he stopped to visit he was extremely kind and compassionate."

"That's what makes a good army officer," Rebecca replied with a smile, not wanting to mention her firsthand experience with an officer who was now buried in the Punchbowl near Honolulu.

"In talking with him just those few minutes it seems like Major Lee has a tremendous background in history. He'll make a good resource person if I have students smarter than I am."

"We need all the friends we can make."

"We haolies have got to stick together for moral support," Rebecca laughed. "It'll make our adjustment to Guam a lot easier."

The pair continued the conversation for over an hour. Finally, Ella Mae looked at her watch. "Oh dear. It's getting late and I've got a lot of lesson plans to make before tomorrow. Tomorrow you're invited to my apartment for soft drinks after work."

❧

Edith Dutton waited eagerly at the nurses' station of the Rocky Bluff Care Center for the activities director. Within moments Liz Chapman was inviting her into the office.

"Edith, it's good to see you again. I've heard by the grapevine that you've been doing a lot of contacting for us."

"People have been extremely accommodating and I have a tentative schedule of performers for every Monday, Wednesday, and Friday from now until Christmas," Edith explained as she took a folded piece of paper from her purse and handed it to Liz.

Liz smiled as she scanned the list. "I see you have a lot

of local talent here."

"Oh, yes," Edith smiled. "I contacted the music teacher, Ed Summer, and he was extremely interested. He thought it would build his students' self-confidence to perform before an appreciative audience."

"You're amazing," the activities director replied. "You're one of the few people who is truly intergenera-tional and sees the importance of each stage of life. I hope your enthusiasm is contagious."

"It will be," Edith replied. "Everyone must grow older and after experiencing the entire life cycle one can't help but gain the intergenerational perspective."

"I understand you organized the Mothers Encouraging Moms group at your church," Liz said. "That's one of the best examples of one generation helping another that I've ever heard of."

Edith smiled. "The response has been good. Both the mothers and grandmothers have become extremely committed to helping each other. Now we want to expand to include the great-grandmothers," she explained. "Many of them are here in the care center."

"That's perfect. The residents enjoy the visits of younger people and those who are able like to get out and mingle with the rest of the community." Liz could scarcely contain her excitement.

"Teresa Lennon has been working on that part of our outreach," Edith explained. "I'll have her get in touch with you and see what can be worked out."

"Edith, I can't tell you how much I appreciate all you're doing for the care center," Liz declared as she gave her older friend a hug.

"The feelings are mutual," Edith replied. "I can't thank you enough for all you've done for Roy. I was so afraid he'd feel neglected when I had to place him here, but with all the loving care he gets, he's adjusted extremely well."

Edith then left the office and went to Roy's room. Her visits had become routine. She first greeted him, read a couple chapters from the Bible, read the important sections of the newspaper and letters and caught him up on the happenings of the family and community. By that time Roy would fall asleep and Edith would work on her knitting until Dan Blair came to give her a ride home. She was happy if Roy made even the slightest attempt to communicate.

❧

After the cause of the Reeds' fire was determined and a warrant was issued for Dick's arrest, life returned to normal for Chief Hatfield. He spent at least ten hours a day at the fire station. He went to his weekly Lions' Club meeting and church on Sundays. However, the after events of the fire had opened a part of his life that he never knew existed. He had shared the early frustrating hours of investigating that fire with an understanding woman. When his beloved aunt had died that same woman was there to help him through the grieving process. Now that the crisis was over he longed to share the routine of life with her, but she was fifteen thousand miles away.

This weekend I think I'll surprise Rebecca and call her. I'm going to need to do some exact calculations to get my time right. Andy pondered for a few minutes and made some scratches on his notepad. *They are one day ahead of us minus eight hours for daylight time. If I call around nine o'clock Saturday night it would be one p.m. Sunday afternoon on Guam.* Andy could hardly wait for Saturday night to come. This was going to be one of the most unpredictable things he had done in his life.

The next Sunday afternoon Rebecca returned from church, changed into her favorite pair of shorts, and fixed herself a hamburger with all the trimmings. She took her plate onto the balcony of her apartment and watched the children in the playground across the street. The tropical breeze blew through her hair. Suddenly the relaxing scene was interrupted by the shrill ring of the phone. She hurriedly pushed back the screen door and ran to the phone.

"Hello."

"Hello, Rebecca. How are you?"

Rebecca paused. *The voice is familiar, but it couldn't be,* she thought. *Maybe if I keep talking I can figure out who it is.*

"I'm doing fine. How are you doing?"

"Rebecca, you still don't know who this is, do you?"

"You sound so much like a friend in Montana but I really can't tell."

Andy laughed. "This is your friend in Montana, Andy Hatfield. It's been several weeks since I've heard from you and wondered how things were going."

"Oh! Andy, thank you for calling. I'm so homesick I could cry. To answer your question, it was a hard adjustment at first," Rebecca admitted, "but except for being lonesome, I'm beginning to get settled in."

"I'm glad to hear things are going better. Have you made any new friends?"

"The head of the English Department has kind of taken me under her wing. She's a native Chamorro who was educated in Portland so she has a pretty good understanding of both cultures. Her daughter who's a senior has been working in the library as a student aide so I'm getting personally involved with the entire family."

Andy smiled. "That was one of the reasons you wanted

to go to Guam."

"It's a broadening experience for me, that's for sure," Rebecca replied. "A young teacher from South Carolina lives across the hall. This is her first teaching assignment and it's quite a struggle for her. She's in the toughest high school on the island and she lacks the experience and self-confidence to meet the demands."

"I imagine you're taking her under your wing the way Edith Dutton has helped most of the struggling young people in Rocky Bluff," Andy said.

"I'm trying," Rebecca admitted, "but I'd never be able to match Edith's achievements. She has so much wisdom and understanding."

"Although she always appears poised and in control, she's had many heartaches in her life," Andy reminded her. "I'm sure that's how she developed her compassion for others."

"Not to change to the subject, but what do you hear from the high school? I really miss Grady Walker and all the other people there."

"Everything seems to be going well. The football team has won most of its games," Andy explained. "Ryan Reynolds suffered a sprained ankle and had to sit out a few games, but he's back in action as good as ever. I don't think the football team is good enough to make it to the state tournaments this year, but everyone is counting on the basketball team going all the way to the top."

"There are high school football and basketball teams here, but the main sport is soccer. I'm getting to be a real fan of our local team, especially the girls."

"Have you heard the outcome of the Reed fire?" Andy asked.

"No, I often wondered what happened to Dick Reed," Rebecca replied. "The first few weeks I was here I received a lot of letters from Rocky Bluff, but they're getting few and far between now."

"We couldn't find the exact cause of the fire so we called the state crime lab to help us. Marty Sanchez was here the next day. His brilliance never ceases to amaze me," Andy explained.

"So don't keep me in suspense," Rebecca chided. "What caused the fire?"

"It didn't take long for Marty to determine that the thermostat on the space heater in the hallway had been removed. Also, the heater had been laying on its side on top of a child's receiving blanket. To add to that, Dick had taken out a million dollar insurance policy on Anita just three months prior to the fire. Needless to say, there's a warrant out for Dick's arrest, but no one knows where he is."

"Hasn't he even tried to contact his two remaining children?" Rebecca queried.

"Anita's parents haven't heard from him since they brought the children back to Spokane with them," Andy explained. "It's all pretty strange."

"It's hard for me to believe that Dick Reed would be capable of murder," Rebecca replied. "He seemed to be such a strong family man."

"That's what we thought until we started checking his background," Andy replied. "It seems that he was married before and his first wife died mysteriously in a boating accident. Nothing was ever proven, but he had just taken out a large life insurance policy on her right before the boating accident also."

Rebecca looked worried. "Do the police have any clues at all?"

"He simply turned the running of the motel over to the

handyman and disappeared. He's now on the FBI's most wanted list, but he seems to have vanished into thin air. The longer he's gone the less likely it'll be that we'll find him."

Andy took a deep breath before continuing. "Rebecca, I don't want this conversation to end on a downer," he said. "I wanted to let you know that amidst that tragedy there was a good thing that came out of it."

"What's that?"

"I discovered that I enjoy being with you," Andy replied. "I just regret that it took so long for me to realize that I occasionally need female companionship. When I finally did, you were half a world away."

Rebecca's heart raced. "I feel much the same way," she replied. "Two years seems like a long time to be gone."

"I know," Andy sighed. "Maybe there'll be a way we can get together next summer. Right now it doesn't seem realistic, but stranger things have happened."

"You don't know how much I'd like that, but I signed a two-year contract and I can't let GCA down. The library is just beginning to take shape." Rebecca chuckled. "Maybe you could use some of those weeks of vacation time you've accumulated through the years."

"Don't laugh. Maybe I will."

seven

"Mom, I hope you'll be able to be at the store for our fortieth anniversary sale," Bob Harkness said as he relaxed in his mother's living room. "We're planning to have a big media blitz the week before, with ads in the paper and on TV and radio. We'll be serving the customary coffee, punch, and cookies, and I was wondering if you'd be there to greet people."

"I'd love to," Edith smiled. "It doesn't seem like its been forty years since your father first opened for business."

"It's seen a lot of changes through the years," Bob replied. "I guess the biggest tribute to Dad is when we opened the satellite store in Running Butte, and Jean and Jim returned to Montana to run it."

"I thought when they moved to Idaho I'd only get to see them once or twice a year, and I would be just a voice on the telephone to my grandchildren. It is so nice to have them less than a hundred miles away."

Bob stretched out his legs and placed them on the footstool. "They're planning on being here for the big sale," he explained. "Larry Reynolds is more than capable of handling things without them. In fact, it won't be long before we might want to consider opening a third store and have him manage that one."

Edith beamed. "That'd be exciting. Not only from the business point of view but from Larry's position. We've sure have been through a lot with him through the years. He's grown from a rebellious sports star and abusive husband to a solid family man and business manager."

"Yes, and most of those changes have come about because of your influence."

"I haven't done anything out of the ordinary. I just happened to be in the right place at the right time." Edith took a deep breath as her mind raced back through the years. "I didn't choose to be the first one into the school office after he shot the principal. A few years later it was just a coincidence that it was my night to answer the crisis line when his wife called begging for help."

"Mom, stop being so modest. Anyone else would have panicked, but you had the calming words to defuse a hostile situation. You not only took care of the crisis, you followed up and became their friend and mentor, always expecting the best out of them."

"Through the years of teaching I've discovered that if you have high expectations for people they will generally rise to the challenge. If you don't expect them to amount to anything, they won't," Edith explained.

"With that philosophy I can see why they named the new wing of the high school after you." Bob became silent as he stared out the picture window for several minutes.

"Mom, I'm afraid I'm not nearly as good a parent as you and Dad were," he muttered.

Edith studied her son's face, trying to understand the depth of his concern. "You have two beautiful teenage children," she protested.

"That I do, but they both have a mind of their own."

"You wouldn't want it any other way, would you?" Edith countered.

"Well, I was hoping that Jay would enroll in the business college at the University of Montana, but all he can talk about is joining the Air Force as soon as he graduates."

"What's wrong with that?"

"Dad worked hard to start this store and I was hoping we could pass it on to the next generation of Harknesses."

"The thing your dad would have liked the most is for his grandchildren to follow their own dreams and set their own course in life."

"I know, but I've always felt that joining the military out of high school was only for those who didn't have the ability to go on to college."

Edith smiled. "You've been too absorbed in that store to see what's going on with the career choices of young people lately," she chided. "Many use the military as a way to an education, not a way to escape it. Let Jay make his own decisions and he'll be okay."

"You're probably right," Bob sighed, "but it seems so unnatural to have a daughter who's more interested in the hardware business than a son. It's amazing to watch Dawn tinker with the broken lawn mowers that come in. At fourteen I think she knows how to use every tool in the store."

"Maybe she's your answer to keeping the store in the family," Edith replied. "Who says a woman can't successfully run a business? I was afraid to try when your father died, but times are different now. Businesswomen are finally obtaining their due respect."

Bob smiled as he again gazed out the front window. His mother always seemed to have the right words to keep the struggles of day-to-day life in perspective.

❧

"Ella Mae, it looks like school must be going better for you," Rebecca said as she met her neighbor on the steps to their apartment building.

"Oh, yeah," Ella Mae grinned. "I only had two discipline referrals today. Why don't you stop over at my apartment and I'll update you on the exciting happenings of GW High School."

The change in Ella Mae's mood was enough to peak Rebecca's curiosity as she followed the young teacher into her one-bedroom apartment. "Okay, what gives?" Rebecca teased. "Discipline referrals don't bring that kind of grin."

"Seriously," Ella Mae tried to protest. "My classroom control is getting better, but I don't think it's because of my great teaching ability."

"What else could it be?"

"Major Lee spotted my frustrations right away. He also noticed that the ring leaders were in his ROTC program and that was all it took."

Rebecca looked puzzled. "What difference would that make?"

"A lot," Ella Mae laughed. "Instead of writing a referral to the office where they could sit in the detention room and sleep for an hour or two, I send them to Major Lee. No one likes that. He has them running laps and doing push-ups. My discipline problems are down seventy-five percent and the principal thinks I'm a great teacher to have the students under such good control."

Rebecca broke into gales of laughter. "It may not be the conventional way of doing things, but nothings works better than success."

"Major Lee has been stopping by my classroom after school nearly every day. It gives me something to look forward to after a hot, frustrating day," Ella Mae confided.

Rebecca's eyes danced. " O. . .o. . .oh. . . Sounds serious."

"Nothing like that," the young teacher protested. "We're both lonesome and need someone to talk to. He's from

Elberton, Georgia, which is only thirty-five miles from where I grew up in South Carolina. We 'rebels' have to stick together. There's few of us left."

"I bet you still sing 'Dixie' every day," Rebecca teased.

"Naah. . . They outlawed that a long time ago."

Rebecca's voice became serious. "Has Major Lee been on Guam long?"

"This is his second year of a two-year contract," Ella Mae replied. "He's already counting the days until he can go home. His brother wants him to come back to Georgia so they can go into the publishing business together. Now he wishes he would have returned as soon as he retired from active duty, but he'd never served in the Pacific before and found the possibility of coming to Guam intriguing."

"He sounds interesting," Rebecca said. "I'd like to meet him sometime."

"I'm sure you'd like him. We were planning on attending the Christmas parade. Why don't you come with us?

"I wouldn't want to intrude on your date," Rebecca protested.

"It's not a date. A group of stateside teachers from GW were planning on going together and making it a day."

Rebecca looked at her friend with interest. "In that case, where and when is it?"

"It's the Friday after Thanksgiving. The entire island turns out and they block off Marine Drive for part of the day. They say the floats made from palm fronds are beautiful. I'd really like you to join us. It should be a lot of fun," Ella Mae insisted.

"Thanks," Rebecca smiled. "I wouldn't miss it for the world."

"Major Lee is making arrangements for us to go to

Tarrague Beach at Anderson Air Force Base after the parade. He says that's one of the perks he gets for having stayed in the army for twenty years."

"Mitzi was telling me about that beach," Rebecca replied. "They say it's the most beautiful one on the island, but the locals don't have access to it since it's on a military reservation."

Ella Mae shrugged her shoulders. "I don't know anything about that. I'm just anxious to see the beach. Our gym teacher is planning on bringing a volleyball and net and we're all chipping in on the food."

"Let me know what I can bring," Rebecca replied as she rose to leave. As she returned to her own apartment Rebecca became pensive. *I've spent most of my time here thinking about how lonely I am and how much I miss Rocky Bluff. I haven't ventured further than the school, church, and grocery store. If I'm going to take fullest advantage of my time on Guam I've got to experience more of the culture and see more of the sights.*

The next morning when Rebecca signed in at the school office there was a poster on the bulletin board.

EVERYONE'S INVITED TO THE ALL
SCHOOL FIESTA THANKSGIVING DAY
FROM NOON—??. PLEASE SEE MITZI
QUINATA FOR MENU SUGGESTIONS.

Rebecca's interest was peaked. She had heard of Mexican fiestas, but never a Guamanian fiesta. She hurried to the library and began setting up for the day. It wasn't long before the door opened.

"Hi, Rebecca. Are you coming to the Thanksgiving Day Fiesta?" Mitzi asked.

"Perhaps," Rebecca said as she laid a stack of books on the table. "I'm anxious to learn more about it."

"We want to make our stateside teachers and students feel welcome. I know it must be hard to be away from your families during the holiday season so we're throwing the fiesta in your honor. You don't have to bring a thing. We want to share some of our Guamanian dishes with you."

"What's different here than on the mainland?" Rebecca queried.

"By eating in the school cafeteria you've already experienced our red rice," Mitzi explained. "We have our own version of southern spareribs. You won't want to miss out on our chicken *kelaguen* which combines coconut, chicken, onion, peppers, salt, and lemon juice. However, there's one dish I want to warn you about and that's *finadene*. It's a very, very hot sauce using deceivingly small Guamanian peppers. The kids like to coax the newcomers into taking a mouthful of it and then sit back and watch the reactions."

Rebecca laughed. "Thanks for the warning. I'll be suspicious of any sauce the kids are too anxious for me to try."

As Rebecca went about her daily tasks her sense of isolation was replaced by the sense of adventure which she once felt when she first began considering coming to Guam. Instead of being alone for the holidays she had many new friends to share the festivities with.

⠌⠁

"Fetch it, Shu-shu," Jeffey Blair shouted as he threw the rubber ball across the front lawn for the Pekingese to retrieve. Shu-shu scampered across the lawn, picked up the ball, and dropped it at Jeffey's feet. Jeffey took the ball and threw it again. At first the game was fun for the five-year-old, but it didn't take long for its repetitiveness to become boring. Seeing his dad raking leaves on the other side of the drive, Jeffey could not resist the three-foot pile. He took a running jump into the very center. Leaves flew everywhere.

"Jeffey, I've been working all afternoon trying to get these raked before the first snowfall," Dan scolded light-heartedly. "I don't want them scattered all over the lawn again."

Dan's words were lost in the crisp autumn air as Jeffey took another flying leap into the pile. As Jeffey lay giggling in the leaves a screech of tires echoed from the street, accompanied by a loud yelp. A car door slammed as Dan and Jeffey ran toward the curb where Shu-shu lay shaking on the side of the street. His back leg twisted into contortions. Chief Hatfield knelt beside the stricken dog and shook his head.

"It doesn't look good," he said to Dan.

Dan nodded in agreement as he put his arm around his son.

"It's my fault, Daddy," Jeffey sobbed. "I was supposed to watch Shu-shu and keep her out of the street. If anything happens to her Rebecca will really be mad at me."

"Let's take her to the vet and see if Doc Howe can fix her up," Chief Hatfield said. "I really feel bad about this."

Dan hurried to the back porch and found an old blanket. Gently he wrapped the dog in the quilt and climbed into the back seat of the fire chief's car, followed closely by his crying son. Chief Hatfield took a shortcut across town to the animal clinic. Fortunately, when they arrived Doc Howe was just returning from the Reynolds' ranch where he'd been vaccinating cows.

"What happened here?" Doc Howe asked as he surveyed the bundle in Dan's arms and the sobbing child beside him.

"I'm afraid I wasn't watching close enough and the dog ran into the street in front of me," Chief Hatfield explained. "I hope you'll be able to fix her up. She belongs to Rebecca Sutherland and Jeffey was taking care of her while she's on Guam."

"We'll have to take some x-rays and see what's broken," Doc Howe said as he motioned for Dan to bring the dog to the examining room. "The way she's shivering I'm afraid she's going into shock."

As Shu-shu laid on the table each breath became further and further apart until there was no movement at all.

"I'm afraid she's gone," Doc Howe said softly. "Would you like me to take care of her?"

"I'd appreciate it if you would," Chief Hatfield replied. "Would you be able to have her buried at the pet cemetery on Boot Hill? I'm sure that's what Rebecca would want."

"No problem at all," the veterinarian assured them. "I'll have a wooden marker made with her name and date of death."

"What am I going to tell Rebecca when she comes home?" Jeffey sobbed. "I promised her I'd take good care of her dog."

Andy put his arm around the boy. "Don't worry about a thing. I'll call her this weekend and tell her it was all my fault. I should have been watching closer as I pulled away from the Reeds' home."

"I should be responsible for the long distance call," Dan protested.

"No problem," Chief Hatfield replied. "I wanted an excuse to call her anyway. I just didn't want it to be one with bad news."

That Saturday evening Andy dialed Rebecca's number on Guam. He waited as he heard a number of clicks on the line and then ringing.

"Hello," a soft voice answered.

"Hello, Rebecca. How are you?"

"Andy, this time I know your voice."

"It's amazing that our connection is as clear as if we were just across town," Andy responded.

"They say that when they laid the fiber-optic cable to Guam a few years ago it made a big difference in the telephone reception" Rebecca explained. "Before the cable, the signal had to be beamed to a satellite and back down so it was subject to a lot of weather interference. Now it just zips along on the cable."

"You're definitely on the information super highway now," Andy chuckled.

"So much the better for keeping up on the Rocky Bluff news," Rebecca replied as floods of memories engulfed her. "What's going on there?"

Andy took a deep breath. "I have some bad news for you. There was an accident in front of your house and I'm afraid I'm the one who's responsible."

"What happened?"

"I went to the Reeds' house to secure it before winter set in," the fire chief explained. "When I was leaving I saw Jeffey playing with Shu-shu in your yard. All of a sudden the dog darted in front of my car and I didn't have time to stop. We took her to the vet's, but it was too late. I had her buried at the pet cemetery on Boot Hill. I'm really sorry."

There was a long pause before Rebecca replied. "Those things happen. Did Jeffey see the whole thing?"

"I'm afraid he did and he blamed himself for not watching the dog closer, but there was nothing he could have done. I think he cried for hours."

"I feel so bad for him," Rebecca sighed. "He has such a tender spirit and hurts so easily. I'll call him and let him know that I don't hold him responsible. I appreciate you calling and letting me know."

"I wanted an excuse to call you anyway, but I'm sorry it had to be bad news. I'm anxious to know how things are going on Guam."

Rebecca began telling about her experiences at her first Guamanian fiesta, the Christmas parade, and her trip to Tarrague Beach. "The strangest part of the holidays here is seeing Santa and his sleigh on top of a palm tree," she giggled. "Everyone seems to take it as normal while I nearly laugh out loud every time I see one."

While the conversation continued in a jovial vein, the bond of commonality and depth of understanding grew with each passing moment. When they finally hung up the phone, Rebecca smiled to herself. *Mother used to tell me that 'Absence makes the heart grow fonder' was just a cliché and it never happens that way, but this time I think Mother was wrong. The longer I'm away from Rocky Bluff the fonder I'm becoming of Andy.*

eight

"Dawn, do you think you'd be able to sing here at the care center sometime this month?" Edith queried as her fourteen-year-old granddaughter pulled up a chair beside her step-grandfather.

"I'd be glad to," Dawn replied, "but I'll have to have clearance from the principal."

Edith smiled as the face of her former employer flashed before her. "I'll give Grady Walker a call. He's been extremely cooperative in excusing the students to perform here."

Dawn turned her attention back to her grandfather. "Would you like me to sing for you and your friends?"

Roy smiled and squeezed Dawn's hand. He tried to talk but his words were inaudible.

Dawn turned her attention back to her grandmother. "I never get nervous when I perform here," she confided. "These people make me feel so welcome and appreciate everything I do, despite how bad I might sound."

"I've been extremely pleased with the community's response to my request for local talent," Edith said. "Even the fire chief has consented to come and play his accordion."

Dawn giggled. "You mean Andy Hatfield has musical ability? He always appeared as an athletic junkie to me."

"I've never heard him myself, but those who have say he has quite a repertoire of the golden oldies," Edith explained. "Those are the kind the residents seem to enjoy the most."

82

Dawn stayed for fifteen more minutes and shared the activities that were going on at the high school.

"Grandma, if you'd excuse me, I'd like to visit some of the others. There are a couple of ladies on the next wing I've gotten kind of attached to."

Edith beamed as she watched her granddaughter leave the room. *It's refreshing to see interest in other generations spreading throughout Rocky Bluff. I hate to see each age group become isolated.*

❧

"Rebecca, what are you planning to do over Christmas vacation?" Ella Mae asked as the two relaxed on the patio of Rebecca's apartment.

"I thought it might be a good time to take in some local flavor," Rebecca replied. "For a beginning I wanted to go boonie stomping through the jungle and visit Talafofo Falls."

"Sounds like fun." Ella Mae watched the children in the playground below before continuing. "Major Lee is planning on flying back to Georgia to help his brother. They'd like to be able to open their doors for business as soon as he gets back in June. He's going to take some Christmas presents back to my family in South Carolina."

"Why don't we plan to do something special together while we have the free time?" Rebecca queried.

"Major Lee said I shouldn't return to the mainland without first visiting Saipan. He says there's a lot of World War Two relics there and an old jail where it's rumored that Amelia Earhardt and her navigator were held by the Japanese before they died."

"Hmmm. I never thought about island hopping," Rebecca replied. "The other Mariannas Islands are only a hundred miles from here. They say the planes that dropped the atomic bombs on Hiroshima and Nagasaki took off from the airstrip on Tinian. That ought to be interesting to see."

Ella Mae was bursting with excitement. "I'll stop at the Visitors' Bureau for travel guides. Major Lee can point out the best places to see and where to stay. This could be the most exciting Christmas vacation we'll ever have."

૨ઢ

After school the next day Ella Mae knocked at Rebecca's door with a handful of travel brochures in her hand.

"Rebecca, look at these," she exclaimed as soon as her friend opened the door. "We've got to take our cameras and stay on Saipan as long as we can. It's dotted with beaches and breathtaking precipices. There's Bird Island and the Grotto which is a sunken pool connecting the ocean by twin underwater passages. I can hardly wait."

"Slow down. Slow down," Rebecca chided. "Let me see what you have."

Ella Mae and Rebecca spread the literature across the kitchen table. Their eyes danced as they surveyed the pictures of secluded sandy white beaches and windsurfers frolicking on the waves. "This is the place for me," Ella Mae announced. "In fact, I've found the perfect hotel to stay at."

"Where's that?"

"Right here at the Pacific Regency," Ella Mae replied as she uncovered a brochure hidden on the bottom of the stack. "Look, it includes twelve acres of lush gardens and international gourmet dining. There's tennis and windsurfing. What else could we want?"

"Fantastic," Rebecca exclaimed. "Let's call the travel agency and make the reservations. "How about flying over the day before Christmas and coming home the second of January?"

Rebecca took the phone and dialed the number on the back of one of the folders. Within minutes they both had given their credit card numbers, and the hotel and flight reservations were confirmed. They began to plan what they would pack. This was going to be their most exciting Christmas vacation ever.

৵

Two weeks later Rebecca and Ella Mae deplaned at the Saipan Airport. Instead of a rolling passenger gate meeting the plane they deplaned into the tropical sun on the landing strip and walked into the nearby terminal. They waited in line to show the Immigration Inspector the necessary paperwork. Although Saipan is a Commonwealth of the United States passports are not needed, and both women were glad they had brought theirs along to expedite their entrance into the terminal. They hurried to the car rental agency near the entrance.

"Hafa adai," Rebecca greeted.

"Hello," the local agent responded. "May I help you?"

"We'd like to rent an economy car until the second of January," Rebecca replied.

"We have just the one you need," the agent replied as he pointed to a small Japanese car parked outside his window.

"That'll be perfect," Ella Mae said as Rebecca began filling out the paperwork.

The two women finished packing their luggage into the small trunk and slid onto the front seat of the car. Rebecca started the engine and they both breathed a sigh of relief as the air conditioner began blowing cool air.

"Ahh. This is the life," Ella Mae uttered as Rebecca steered the car onto the main street.

Both were amazed at the lack of hustle and bustle

compared to Guam. Somehow Saipan had been able to retain the quietude of a getaway island.

"Let's check in at the Pacific Regency and then go exploring," Rebecca said. "Would you look at the map and tell me where to turn?"

Upon arrival at the hotel parking lot Rebecca and Ella Mae took their luggage from the trunk of the car and walked toward the front door. As soon as the door opened in front of her, Rebecca gasped and froze. She immediately jumped backward away from the doorway.

"What's wrong?" Ella Mae asked. "You look like you've seen a ghost."

"I have," Rebecca stammered. "The man working the front desk used to be my next door neighbor. He's accused of setting his house on fire where his wife and two children died. He's wanted in Rocky Bluff on three counts of homicide."

Ella Mae trembled with excitement. "What are you going to do?"

Rebecca's heart raced. "I've got to get to a phone where I can call the mainland."

"I think I saw an International Telephone Center on our way in," Ella Mae replied.

The women hurried across the parking lot, threw their luggage back in the trunk, and jumped into the car. Rebecca retraced her path toward the airport until she saw the phone center sign. They parked the car by the curb and rushed inside. The room was lined with oversized booths.

"Can I make a call to Montana from here?" Rebecca asked the woman behind the desk.

"That's what we're here for," the clerk smiled. "I'll punch in your code for booth twenty-three. It'll record the cost of your call and you can pay as you leave."

Rebecca reached in her purse that contained her address book with Andy's phone number. She closed the door to the booth and punched the necessary thirteen digits. It seemed forever before a familiar voice was on the other end of the line.

"Hello, Andy," Rebecca gasped without waiting for a response. "I just saw Dick Reed."

"You what?" Andy shouted into the phone.

"A friend and I came to Saipan for the holidays. We were about to check in to the Pacific Regency Hotel when I saw Dick behind the desk," Rebecca explained.

"Did he see you?" Andy asked excitedly.

"I don't think so. I stepped back outside the door just as soon as I saw him. What should I do next?"

"The Commonwealth of the Northern Marinas Islands is a part of the United States and the FBI should have an office there. Go to their office and report what you have just seen to the Special Agent in charge. Dick Reed is on the FBI's most wanted list. I'm sure the Special Agent there will recognize his name. If the FBI agent there needs more information have him contact Stuart Leonard, our County Attorney. Just don't let Dick Reed know you're on the island."

"Thanks a lot," Rebecca sighed. "I hope they can catch him and put him away for a long time. I'll try to call you after I've been to the FBI."

The conversation was kept brief and to the point. Rebecca hung up the phone and returned to the counter. "That will be eighteen dollars and thirty-five cents," the clerk said as she checked the monitor and punched the amount into the cash register.

Rebecca handed her a twenty-dollar bill and waited while she counted back the change.

"Is there an FBI office on Saipan?"

"Yes, they're in the same office as the U.S. Attorney in the Horiguchi Building in Garripan," the clerk replied with a quizzical look.

"How do I get there?" Rebecca queried. "I have a map here if you wouldn't mind tracing the route."

The clerk took the map and made a dotted line to the Horiguchi Building. "This should help," she replied as she handed the map back. "It's not hard to find since it's the tallest building on the island."

"Thanks for your help," Rebecca replied as she and Ella Mae hurried out the door.

Upon arriving at the government building Rebecca and Ella Mae consulted the building directory and took the escalator to the third floor. After passing through security they were admitted to the U.S. Attorney's Office. Rebecca asked to see the Special Agent in charge of the FBI office. She was immediately ushered into a small, plain office.

"My name is Eric Grimes. How may I help you?"

Rebecca introduced herself and explained about Dick Reed and the fire. She then went on to tell how she had just seen him at the front desk of the Pacific Regency Hotel and had called the fire chief of Rocky Bluff, Montana, who had suggested she come to see him.

The agent took frantic notes as she was speaking. When he had finished he typed Dick Reed's name into the computer. Instantly his picture, description, and criminal charges appeared on the screen.

"Here's our man," Agent Grimes exclaimed slamming his fist on the desk.

"It's quite common for fugitives to come to the U.S. islands in the Pacific. They are as far away from the mainland as they can possibly be and they can enter without a passport, but I'm going to need an official request from the local police authorities before I can pick him up."

"Our fire chief said you should contact our local county attorney, Stuart Leonard in Rocky Bluff, Montana," she replied. "But it's now late at night in Montana."

"Would Dick Reed recognize you if he saw you again?" Agent Grimes asked.

"Certainly," Rebecca replied. "We were next door neighbors for many years."

"Do you think he saw you at the hotel?"

"I think I stepped back fast enough."

"Good. I recommend you spend the night at another hotel," Eric suggested.

"But we already have reservations at the Pacific Regency," Rebecca protested.

"That's no problem. Let me make some phone calls."

Rebecca and Ella Mae sat quietly while the special agent made two brief calls. After hanging up the phone he turned back to them.

"You're all registered at the Hikishi Hotel just a couple blocks from the Regency. I'll let you know just as soon as we have him in custody and then you can go wherever you like."

"Thanks for your help," Rebecca replied as she rose to leave. "I don't want to have someone who's responsible for the death of his wife and children living in luxury on a tropical island."

When Rebecca and Ella Mae finally checked into their hotel room, Ella Mae collapsed across the bed.

"I said we were going to have the most exciting Christmas ever, but I didn't expect all of this."

"You and me both," Rebecca agreed as she looked at her watch and thought a moment. "It's so late back home I don't dare call Andy now. Let's go get something to eat and I'll call him in the morning and wish him a Merry Christmas."

After a delicious Christmas eve dinner the pair sat on the lanai of the hotel and watched the sun set over the Pacific. The meaning of Christmas for all people took on an even greater significance for Rebecca after interacting with a multitude of cultures within the last five months.

The first thing Christmas morning Rebecca calculated the time difference and dialed the familiar Rocky Bluff telephone number.

"Merry Christmas," Andy greeted.

"Merry Christmas to you," Rebecca echoed. "I hope I called at a good time."

"For you any time is a good time. I was hoping you'd call last night after you'd been to the FBI."

"It would have been too late," Rebecca explained, "and I didn't want to disturb you."

"Don't worry about the time. I never have a problem getting back to sleep. So how's it going?"

"Special Agent Eric Grimes did verify that Dick Reed is his man, but he's waiting to get verification from Stuart Leonard before he picks him up. Christmas is a hard time to carry on business," Rebecca replied. "He made reservations for Ella Mae and me at the Hikishi Hotel and told us to stay away from the Pacific Regency until they have Dick Reed in custody."

The wrinkles on Andy's forehead faded. "I've already talked with Stu and he's so excited about locating Dick he could scarcely contain himself. Call me again as soon as you know more. I'll never be able to thank you enough for what you've done."

Rebecca laughed. "All I've done is come to Saipan for

Christmas break to relax in the sun."

"You've demonstrated all kinds of wisdom ever since the frantic ringing of your doorbell the night of the fire," Andy replied. "Although you're miles away, I feel so close to you."

Rebecca's eyes misted as she shot an embarrassed glance toward Ella Mae who was reading another travel guide. "Andy, I feel the same way. I can hardly wait to see you again. There isn't a day that goes by that I don't think about you and Rocky Bluff. I can't believe it'll be over a year before I can go home again."

"Maybe it will be sooner than you think," Andy replied. "If things continue going the way they are, Stuart Leonard will probably need to have you come back to testify at the trial. We'll just have to see what happens."

Rebecca looked pensive. "If it goes to court I hope it's during summer vacation. I was planning on taking a few courses at the University of Guam this summer, but I could take what I was going to spend on tuition and fly home."

"Who knows. Maybe the court will think your testimony is so vital they'll fly you home to testify," Andy pondered. "Please let me know as soon as you hear from Eric Grimes. I don't care what time it is, night or day. You have my work number so don't hesitate to call me there if I'm not at home."

"Will do," Rebecca promised.

Again the conversation ended on a jovial note of the description of relaxing on the beaches of a tropical paradise. It wasn't as much the words that were shared as it was the unspoken feelings that flowed over the phone lines that added excitement to Rebecca's spirit.

"Love is connected to a telephone wire," she snickered to herself.

Ella Mae watched her older friend as she hung up the phone and stared out the hotel window to the ocean below.

"You seem like you're a thousand miles away," she chided.

"More like seventeen thousand," Rebecca replied as she turned her attention back to her friend. "I'm letting myself do what I said I wouldn't. . .reminiscing about home. What are we going to do tomorrow?"

"There's an announcement in the lobby for snorkeling lessons. It said they'd provide all the gear. Want to give it a try?" Ella Mae coaxed.

"Me snorkel?" Rebecca chided. "There are some things people over fifty just shouldn't do!"

"Perhaps," Ella Mae teased, "but snorkeling isn't one of them. In fact, you're probably in better physical condition than I am."

Rebecca grinned. "Then it's a deal. Tomorrow I'll go make reservations for the two of us. If we do this, I want lots of pictures. No one in Rocky Bluff will believe I had the courage to go snorkeling. In fact, most probably don't even know what it is."

The next two days Rebecca and Ella Mae took advantage of every possible tourist activity available. Rebecca thought she had never had as much fun as she was having, however a nagging worry kept hanging over her. *When will Eric Grimes call about Dick Reed? I don't dare go near the Pacific Regency until this is all over.*

Finally, Friday afternoon when they had just returned from the beach to change before dinner the phone rang.

"Hello," a deep male voice greeted. "May I speak with Rebecca Sutherland?"

"Speaking."

"This is Special Agent Eric Grimes. I just wanted you

to know that I talked with the County Attorney in Rocky Bluff, Montana, and he verified that he was the one who issued the warrant for the arrest of Dick Reed. We now have Mr. Reed in custody and he'll appear before the U.S. District Court in Saipan in two weeks for extradition to Montana. After that, marshals of the U.S. Justice Department will escort him back to Rocky Bluff. You may now travel any place on the island without fear of being spotted by Mr. Reed. I want to thank you for your cooperation. Citizens like you make this job so much easier. If there's anything I can do to make your stay on Saipan more pleasant please let me know."

Rebecca hung up the phone and collapsed on the bed sobbing.

Ella Mae put her hand on Rebecca's shoulder to comfort her. "What's wrong? Can I do anything to help?"

"No," Rebecca smiled through her tears. "I'm just relieved. It's finally over. Dick Reed is behind bars. Justice can now be served."

nine

"Edith, would you like to have dinner with us Sunday?" Dan asked as he drove his older friend home from one of her daily visits to the care center. "We've been so busy during the holiday season that Beth and I haven't had much time to socialize."

"I'd love to," Edith replied. "Besides, I haven't seen Jeffey for several weeks."

Dan smiled mysteriously. "He's been asking about you lately. He has some exciting news for you."

"And you won't tell me what it is, will you?" Edith teased.

"I wouldn't ruin his surprise for anything."

The next Sunday the pew next to Edith was vacant when the Blair family entered the church. Jeffey was the first to spot his adopted grandmother and hurried for the seat beside her. His parents followed close behind.

"Hi, Grandma Edith. Can I sit with you?"

"Sure, honey," Edith responded as she patted the spot next to her. "This seat has your name on it."

"I have a secret," Jeffey whispered, "but I can't tell you until dinner."

"Can you give me a clue?" Edith smiled.

"Just one clue. It has to do with Mommy."

"Is she fixing your favorite food for dinner?"

Jeffey shook his head as the organist began to play the prelude and a quiet hush spread throughout the church.

Edith surveyed the couple. A little more than six months before they had said their wedding vows before this same altar. Dan not only promised to take Beth as his wife, but

Jeffey as his son. The adoption was finalized within days after Dan and Beth's marriage. *I've never seen Beth this radiant,* Edith thought as the congregation stood to sing the opening hymn. *Married life must be good for her.*

That afternoon as Edith and the Blairs finished their dessert around the dining room table in Rebecca Sutherland's home, Edith turned to Jeffey. "When are you going to tell me your secret?"

Jeffey looked questioningly at his mother who nodded her approval. "I'm going to have a new brother," Jeffey announced. "His name's going to be Danny."

Edith reached out and patted Beth's hand. "I'm so happy for all of you. When is he due?"

"The end of June," Beth replied. "Having Dan's child would be the best anniversary present I could possibly have."

"I get to help take care of my new brother," Jeffey announced.

Edith turned her attention back to the proud child. "What if you have a little sister?" she teased.

Jeffey shrugged his shoulders. "That'll be okay. We'll just call her Edith."

Dan flushed. "I guess the secret's out," he sighed. "We wanted to surprise you with the name if a girl was born."

Edith paused. She thought back through all the trials and tribulations she had shared with both Beth and Dan. "I'd be honored, but having a namesake carries a big responsibility to be a role model."

"We know," Dan replied. "Because you're a perfect example of compassion, if we have a girl we want our daughter to bear your name."

Edith shook her head in amusement. "Surely after all these years you've seen my feet of clay."

"Yes, but we also know your feet are grounded on a

solid Rock and you never waiver," Beth replied. "We just want to say thanks for all you've done for us throughout the years."

Edith's eyes misted. "I've grown to love you all as if you were my own flesh and blood." She paused a moment. "Speaking of flesh and blood, I have some other good news for you. Jean and Jim are expecting their second baby about the same time."

"That'll be fun, having the two exactly the same age," Beth beamed. "I'm sure Gloria is as excited about a sibling as Jeffey."

Edith spent the remainder of the afternoon visiting with Beth and Dan and reading stories to Jeffey. Jeffey was already able to identify most of the letters in the alphabet and he enjoyed pointing them out to anyone who took the time to listen.

è

"I finally have Dick Reed locked in our jail," Phil Mooney exclaimed as he entered Chief Hatfield's office in the fire station. "It took the wheels of justice a long time to work, but the federal marshals flew in with him last night on the Treasure State Airlines."

"I imagine Dick wasn't very pleased to be back in Rocky Bluff," Andy replied dryly.

Phil grinned. "I think he was enjoying himself a little too much on Saipan. It was about time his life of leisure ended. Seven months on the loose gave him a false sense of security."

"Stuart Leonard has been working on his prosecution for months. What attorney do you think will defend him?" Andy queried.

"Dick claims he doesn't have any money to hire a lawyer, so Judge Eubanks will have to appoint one," Phil responded. "My guess it will be Dave Wood. He's young and eager to get involved in heavy duty cases."

Andy shook his head. "This would be his first major criminal case. I hope he doesn't get overwhelmed."

"I'm confident he'll do all right," Phil assured him. "He has some close attorney friends in Great Falls and Billings who'll be able to advise him if he gets into trouble."

"I'm glad it's him and not me," Andy retorted. "After all we've been through during the investigation I don't think I could be very objective."

"That's what lawyers are paid for," Phil replied as he looked at his watch. "Guess it's time I get back to the station. They get extremely upset with me if I mess up their lunch schedules."

Andy could hardly wait for Saturday so he could call Rebecca. "Figuring out the time difference is such an inconvenience," he muttered to himself.

Saturday evening Andy dialed Rebecca's number on Guam and waited impatiently for the connection to be made.

"Hello."

"Hello, Rebecca. This is Andy. How are you doing?"

"Andy, it's good to hear your voice again. Until early Saturday morning I was doing great."

Wrinkles creased the fire chief's forehead. "And then what happened?"

"Some teachers and I decided to go boonie stomping through the jungles yesterday," Rebecca laughed. "The vegetation and view of the ocean was beautiful, but now I'm sunburned and covered with mosquito bites. I hurt so bad I couldn't get out of bed to go to church this morning."

Andy chuckled as he pictured her reddened face and arms. "I hope you took lots of pictures. Times like those I'd like to be there to share them with you."

"I wish you were here too. It'd be so much fun to explore the island together," Rebecca said as she rubbed more lotion on her sunburn. "There's so much to do and see, I don't know if I'll get it all taken in by the time my contract is up."

"Maybe you'll want to renew it," Andy teased.

"No way. I miss you and all my friends in Rocky Bluff too much. Don't prolong my suspense. What's the latest news from home?"

"Tuesday the federal marshals brought Dick Reed back to the local jail. It looks like Dave Wood will be defending him."

"Isn't he pretty young and inexperienced to handle a homicide case?" Rebecca queried.

"Few lawyers in this state are experienced with homicide cases. There's just not that many of them. I think he'll do a fine job."

A look of concern spread across Rebecca's face. "How soon will it get to trial?"

"Probably the first week of July. Will it be any problem for you to come back?"

"I'd love to, but I don't think I'll be able to afford it," Rebecca sighed.

"I imagine they'll subpoena you and then the court will pay your transportation. You'll be one of their key witnesses. I'll let you know when I have more of the details from Stuart Leonard."

Rebecca beamed. "I was planning on taking a few courses this summer at the University of Guam just to pass the time, but a trip back would be so much better. I'm getting so homesick I can hardly stand it."

"With that in mind why don't you start marking your calendar? There are only nine weeks left of school and then you can come home for the summer. I'm sure the second school year will be much easier than the first."

"I'll need the second year to reap the fruits of my hard

work of this year. I'm beginning to get used to hearing a mosaic of languages around me," Rebecca admitted. "Even my library automation project is progressing nicely."

"I always knew you could do it. When you started to get cold feet about your capabilities while we were in Hawaii, I realized how dedicated to quality library services you actually were."

Rebecca blushed under her sunburn. "I couldn't have done it without a lot of parent volunteers. Many of the military wives are immersed in their children's school and volunteer all their free time to help in the library."

"That could be either an asset or a liability depending on their objectivity toward their own child," Andy chuckled.

Rebecca smiled. "Fortunately, most of our parents are just here to help and don't try to tell us how to do our jobs. As out of my own element as I am, I don't think I could stand any outside pressure."

"Hang in there," Andy replied. "You'll soon be home for good. Just savor each moment you have there. You may never be able to return once your contract is over."

"I know. That's why I try to go to as many cultural events as possible. A couple weeks ago I went to the Discovery Day Parade and fiesta. I really had a lot of fun and met a lot of the local people."

"I hate to show my ignorance as far as world history, but who did discover Guam?" Andy queried. "Obviously not Columbus."

"On March 6, 1521, Magellan first sighted Guam. Spain then dominated the island for nearly three hundred years." Rebecca hesitated. "I hate to waste your long distance phone call giving you a history lesson. I'll write you a long letter and send you some informational brochures. This place is absolutely fascinating."

"I guess you're right," Andy sighed. "It's just so good

to talk to you again. I'm looking forward to seeing you this summer."

"I can hardly wait," Rebecca replied. "Do take care of yourself."

"Good-bye, dear. I love you."

"I love you too."

Rebecca hung up the phone. *I always thought that love would have to be exactly like what I had with Eric years ago, but love for Andy it is so different, so relaxing. I think I'll write Edith a letter explaining my feelings toward Andy. She, more than anyone, will understand someone loving deeply and then having another love later in life.*

> *Dear Edith,*
>
> *I just hung up from a long conversation with Andy. I miss him so much I can hardly stand it. It's strange how our friendship has developed into love while we're separated. I never thought I'd find anyone like Eric so I figured I'd never fall in love again. Andy is so different from Eric, and yet equally special. Now I can understand how you and George were so happy together all those years and yet when you met Roy you could again develop a loving relationship.*
>
> *How is Roy doing? He was such a vivacious, outgoing person it's hard to see him no longer able to communicate. I know he's getting excellent care, but I know it must be awfully hard for you to be separated.*
>
> *There's a chance I'll be coming home this summer. Andy said that Dick Reed will be going to trial and I'll be one of the key wit-*

nesses. I hope I can see you then. I miss our long, heart-to-heart conversations.

Give my regards to Roy.

Love,
Rebecca

≈

"Mom, Dad," Jay began as he lingered around the kitchen table after dinner. "The Air Force recruiter was at school today. I'm convinced that enlisting in the Air Force is what I want to do after high school."

"Are you sure you don't want to go to college?" Nancy Harkness protested. "If you majored in business you'd be ready to take over the store when your dad retires."

"Dad and I have discussed this before," Jay reminded them. "I want to join the Air Force and see the world outside Montana."

"You could always join R.O.T.C. while you're in college and then you can go into the Air Force as an officer," Nancy continued.

"I know," Jay replied. "The recruiter explained all that to me, but I'd rather join the service now and take classes wherever I'm stationed. This is what I really want to do; I was hoping that I'd have your support."

Nancy looked chagrined. "Of course we'll support you in whatever you choose to do. It's just hard for me to think about you leaving home for good."

"We've got to accept the fact that our first baby has grown up," Bob snickered as he slapped his son on the shoulder. "When are you going to sign up?"

"There's a teacher's in-service day next Friday so we don't have to go to class. I was wondering if you'd come with me to the Air Force recruiting station in Great Falls that day?" Jay queried.

Nancy and Bob exchanged questioning glances. "I think

we could arrange that," Bob replied. "I'll call Larry Reynolds and see if he can take time from the Running Butte store for a couple days. We could spend the night and do some fun things while we're there. It might be the last time we'll get to take a trip together for some time."

"Thanks, Mom, Dad," Jay said as he got up to leave. "You're the greatest. Sorry I have to get back to the gym by seven-thirty. We have a late practice tonight."

As the back door slammed, Bob turned to his wife. Tears were building in Nancy's eyes.

"Nancy, the next few years will be as much a transition time for us as it will be for Jay and Dawn. The ones leaving home are too caught up in the adventure to be lonely; those of us left behind suffer the loneliness."

"I know," Nancy sighed. "I'll have to find another area to devote myself. I remember how hard it was for your mother when she quit teaching. She struggled with it for several months before things came together for her. Through her searching she became one of the most influential women in the community. Everyone seems to turn to her for guidance. If I could only obtain a fraction of her compassion I'd be satisfied."

"Let's give Mom a call and see if she'd like to ride to Great Falls with us," Bob said as he reached for the kitchen phone.

Nancy nodded in agreement while Bob used the automatic dial on the phone and waited.

"Hello."

"Hello, Mother. How are you?"

"I'm doing fine. I'm just curled up with a new book from the library," Edith replied.

"Do you have any special plans for Friday and Saturday?" Bob queried.

Edith sounded puzzled. "That depends. What do you have in mind?"

"Nancy and I were going to take Jay to Great Falls where he's going to enlist in the Air Force. We were going to spend the night and do the town up right. It'll probably be the last trip we'll get to take with him for a long time and we were wondering if you'd like to join us."

"I'd love to," Edith replied and then she hesitated. "I'm afraid I'd better decline. I don't want to be that far away from Roy."

"Is something wrong?"

"It's not a crisis situation, but every time I go in Roy seems to be weaker than the day before. He's losing a lot of weight and the nurses are now having to help feed him," Edith sighed.

"I'm sorry to hear that. The last few times Nancy and I have stopped to see him he was always sleeping so we hadn't realized there was any change."

"I feel so helpless when I'm with him. I just want to share some of my limited strength with him."

"Mom, you're the most selfless person I know."

"Oh, no," Edith protested adamantly. "I struggle with selfishness just like everyone else." Edith paused. "What's amazed me in watching Roy's deteriorating health is the inner peace he's exhibiting. There always seems to be a smile on his face."

"I'm glad a failing body and mind can't take away the presence of our Lord," Bob replied as he remembered his stepfather during his more vibrant years. "That's the one thing I want to leave behind for my own children. Even when he doesn't realize it, Roy is still giving testimony to his faith in Christ."

ten

Mitzi Quinata burst into the library at Guam Christian Academy the following afternoon as soon as the students were dismissed for the day.

"Rebecca," she exclaimed. "What's this I hear about you going home for the summer?"

"The chances are pretty good," Rebecca replied. "But how did you hear so soon?"

"Angela said she heard you talking to the principal this morning," Mitzi giggled. "It pays to have a snoopy daughter in the same school. I don't know what I'll do for information when she graduates."

"It's still not certain, but I may get subpoenaed to testify at a murder trial," Rebecca stated matter-of-factly.

"Ooo. Sounds serious. What happened?"

"The guy next door decided he loved insurance money more than his wife and four kids. He set his house on fire and his wife and two of the children died."

Mitzi shook her head. "Sounds like a mean dude."

"Surprising enough, he was extremely soft-spoken." Rebecca sunk wearily into her chair. "He was the last person on earth I would have expected to do something like that."

"I guess one never knows what goes on in another's mind," Mitzi sighed, shaking her head. "Did you have nightmares about the fire after it happened or did coming to Guam help remove the memories?"

"I wish I could have left the memories behind, but during Christmas vacation on Saipan I saw my neighbor working in one of the hotels. I reported him to the FBI and they arrested him. No matter where I go I can't seem to get away from it."

"I hope it works out that you get to go home for the summer," Mitzi said, "but I'm afraid once you get home you won't want to come back."

"No chance of that," Rebecca replied. "When I sign a contract and give my word, I have every intention of fulfilling it. Besides it'll take at least another six months to finish automating the school library."

"I admire your dedication. The Academy is fortunate to have you."

"It's been quite a learning experience for me. I'm glad I took the risk and came. It's been worth every minute of frustration that I've had."

The two women glanced at the clock while the janitor noisily pushed his cart into the library. "I better be getting home," Mitzi noted. "I don't have any idea what I'll fix for dinner and my family is used to eating at six o'clock sharp."

Rebecca finished shutting down the computers and locking the video cabinet and then said goodnight to the janitor. A warm tropical breeze blew against her face as she left the air-conditioned library. In the distance she could see the ocean waves lapping against the sandy beach. A surge of homesickness swept over her.

I can't begin to feel sorry for myself, she mused. *In just a few short weeks I'll be back in Montana. I'm sure I won't be nearly as lonely here during my second year.*

≈

The Lewistown High School gym was crowded with spectators from Lewistown and Rocky Bluff. The Class A

District basketball championship game was about to begin. "Daddy, do you think we'll win?" five-year-old Jeffey asked.

"I sure hope so," Dan Blair replied. "Last year we only lost by one point so the team has vowed revenge for this game. They want to go to state in the worst way."

Just then Dan saw Larry and Libby Reynolds enter the gym. Dan stood and motioned for them to join him.

"You're a long ways from Running Butte," he chided as he reached out to shake Larry's hand.

"This is our big night out," Larry replied. "The kids are sleeping over at Jean and Jim's tonight. They wanted to be here to watch Jay play but someone had to keep the store open."

"Only in Montana would someone drive one hundred and fifty miles one way to see a high school basketball game," Dan teased.

"They would if his kid brother was following in his footsteps and taking his team to the state championship," Larry chuckled.

Dan slapped his friend on the shoulder. "A lot has happened since you took Rocky Bluff High School to the state championship in Billings."

"A lot of it I'd like to forget," Larry replied. "I can't imagine that I ever thought playing basketball at the college level was so important that I'd shoot the principal when he disciplined me. I hope my little brother has better priorities than I had."

"You've come a long way since then and have become a model for the current team," Beth encouraged.

Larry nodded. "I owe a lot to the people of Rocky Bluff for forgiving me and accepting me for what I am today and not for what I used to be."

"Just listen to the crowd," Dan declared. "There's more pressure on those kids than on a professional team. The pros play for money while these kids play for community acceptance."

The roar of the crowd increased as the Lewistown high school band began to play their school song. The host teams fans cheered while the visiting team waiting politely for their school song. From the first tip off, electricity filled the gym. By the end of the first quarter it was obvious which team was dominating. Ryan Reynolds and Jay Harkness of Rocky Bluff were at their best. Even though they were both double teamed most of the time, their accuracy at the hoop could not be matched.

The Lewistown fans became quieter and quieter as the point spread between the teams went from two and then five. When the final buzzer sounded, the Rocky Bluff Rams led by ten points. The Rams lifted their leading scorer, Ryan Reynolds, to their shoulders while he cut the traditional victory net from the hoop. No one could have been prouder of their team than former star Larry Reynolds.

"Are you going to Billings next week for the championship games?" Larry asked Dan as the cheering began to subside and the crowd surged towards the exits.

"I'd like to," Dan replied, "but it's my turn to work the crisis lines. Will you be there?"

"I wouldn't miss it for the world. In fact, I'm planning to personally host a celebration for the team whether they win or lose. I don't want them to do what my team did after the final game. . .go out and party."

Dan smiled. "Sounds like a great idea. I'm sure the school officials will appreciate your efforts."

"It's the least I can do."

"Mom, would you like to ride to Billings with us for the state tournaments?" Bob Harkness asked as Edith joined them for Sunday dinner the day after the district basketball finals. "Jay played a fabulous game last night and the state championship game is going to be even better."

Edith turned to her grandson. "Jay, you know how much I've enjoyed watching your sporting events through the years. I hate missing the biggest game of your high school career, but Roy is so bad now I'd hate to leave town for fear he'd take a turn for the worst. I'll be sure to listen to the game on the radio and I hope I can get a copy of the coach's videotape and watch it when you get home."

Jay patted his grandmother's arm. "I understand, Grandma. I'm sure Beth Blair wouldn't mind making a duplicate of the video for you in the school library. She's getting pretty good with the audiovisual equipment."

"I'd appreciate it," Edith smiled. "I'll be sure to give Beth a blank tape to use. In the meantime I'll keep you and the entire team in my prayers. We don't want any repeat of the championship game a few years ago."

Jay chuckled. "We could use all the prayers we can get, but thanks to Larry Reynolds you don't have to worry about a repeat. He's planning a post-game victory dinner whether we win or lose. He's making sure we all keep our priorities straight."

"All the parents are breathing a sigh of relief," Nancy sighed. "We want our kids to have a good time without destroying their futures."

Wednesday afternoon the Rocky Bluff basketball team filled one school bus while the pep band filled another. A score of supporters lined their cars behind the buses. When everyone was ready, Philip Mooney led the procession to the city limits in his patrol car with its lights flashing and siren wailing. Passersby waved and motorists honked their horns. A spirit of jubilation and pride filled the city.

In the Billings Metra the Rocky Bluff Rams won the first three elimination games with ease. The combination of Jay and Ryan could not be stopped. Jay was high scorer in one game and Ryan led in the other two. In the championship game the Rams were paired against the Miles City Bisons.

Larry and Libby Reynolds sat with Bob Harkness. "Did you remember to bring the sheet of team statistics from Sunday's paper?" Bob asked Larry.

"I have it in my pocket," Larry laughed, "but I don't need it. I've got the whole thing memorized. The Bisons' number fifty-five is their top scorer while number twenty-three is their best rebounder. Their point guard is the one to watch out for, though. He doesn't shoot much, but he's a magnificent ball handler."

"Sounds like our boys have their work cut out for them tonight," Bob observed.

"Yes, but I have confidence in them. They're on a roll and I don't think anything can stop them tonight."

The championship teams were evenly matched. First the Bisons led and then the Rams. The roar of the crowd in the Billings Metra was deafening. The pep bands and the cheerleaders helped keep the intensity at a high pitch. The score was tied at seventy-eight with thirty seconds left in the game.

The referee's whistle penetrated the roar of the crowd. He motioned that a foul was called against number twenty-three on the Bisons. Ryan Reynolds was on the free throw line for the Rams. His first shot hit the rim and bounced back. The Rams fans sighed and held their breath while their star took aim for the second shot. The ball teetered on the rim and fell through the net. The Metra was filled with cheers. The Bisons took the ball and raced down the court. The Rams used their best defense and kept their opponents mid-court. With five seconds left in the game, number fifty-five broke loose and shot. Everyone held their breath as the ball neared the hoop. It hit the rim and bounced down. Jay grabbed the rebound and was dribbling down the court when the final buzzer sounded. The Rocky Bluff Rams had won seventy-nine to seventy-eight.

"That was some game," Larry sighed as he relaxed back in his seat, "but it was a little too close for comfort."

"Well, at least we won," Bob shrugged. "Are you ready to go?"

"No way. They're going to have the presentation of the trophies in a few minutes," Larry replied. "The championship trophy will be a welcome addition to the school's trophy case."

The crowd became quiet as a middle-aged man dressed in a sports shirt and slacks walked to the center of the gym floor carrying a portable microphone. Behind him two teenagers pushed a cart bearing five trophies. One by one he called the teams to the floor. First the fourth place team, then the third place, the second place Miles City Bisons and finally the Class A Montana State Champions—the Rocky Bluff Rams.

The Rocky Bluff pep band played the school song as their team ran onto the floor to accept the trophy. When the cheers subsided the master of ceremonies again took the microphone. "And now for the most coveted honor of the tournament," he said, "the Most Valuable Player Award."

The crowd held their breath with anticipation. Each fan had their own selection. Would their favorite be the winner?

"And now the Most Valuable Class A Basketball Player by unanimous decision of the board is. . .Ryan Reynolds of the Rocky Bluff Rams."

Tears rolled unashamedly down Larry's cheeks as his younger brother went forward to accept the honor. His long road back to respectability had been worth it all. Larry's influence on his brother and teammates helped them taste the sweetness of victory while maintaining their priorities and integrity. Tonight Rocky Bluff had many things to celebrate. This night would be chiseled in the history book of Rocky Bluff, Montana.

≥∙

Attorney Dave Wood walked slowly back to his modest office at the edge of town. *Why did Judge Eubanks pick me to defend Dick Reed? There are several more experienced attorneys in Little Big Horn County. I've never handled a homicide case before. The biggest case I've had was the burglary at the lumber yard,* he mused. *Where should I begin?*

Dave turned the corner and walked toward the police station. Maybe Philip Mooney would be able to help him. Dave greeted the receptionist and dispatcher on duty and headed for Phil's office.

"Dave, come in," Phil greeted as he looked up from his pile of paperwork. "Have a seat. What brings you out on such a nice day?"

"I guess I need a little help," he sighed. "Judge Eubanks just appointed me as defense attorney for Dick Reed. I feel extremely inadequate for such a challenge."

"I'm sure you'll do a good job," Phil assured him. "Remember, not many attorneys in Montana have experience with homicide cases. I'll pull the file and you can begin familiarizing yourself with it. There's a little room in the back you can use."

"Thanks," Dave grinned. "I appreciate that. I want to read the file before I meet with Dick. I need to make sure I can make the best decisions for him, given the extreme circumstances and community sentiment."

Phil reached into the file cabinet and handed Dave a bulging manila folder. "Take your time. If you have any questions, be sure and ask."

Dave retreated to the back office furnished only with two straight back chairs and a desk. A small banker's lamp graced the desk. One hour passed and then two. Dave only left the desk to refill his coffee mug. The file was more fascinating than any mystery novel. *What motivates a person like this?* he mused. *My only hope is convincing Dick to plead innocent by reason of insanity.*

Two and a half hours later Dave closed the folders and walked to the police captain's office.

"Thanks for letting me read the file. Would it be possible to talk with Dick now?"

"Sure," Phil agreed. "Let me get the keys."

Phil unlocked the iron gate. Dave shuddered as the metal door clanged shut behind them. *So this is what the inside of a jail looks like,* the young attorney pondered. *If this doesn't scare anyone straight, I don't know what will.*

"Wait here," Phil directed as he pointed to a chair in the jail interview room. "I'll bring Dick to you."

Dave paced around the narrow room until Phil appeared with Dick on the other side of the barred wall.

"Hello, Dick. I'm Dave Wood. How are you doing?"

"How would anyone be doing locked up like this?"

Dave took a deep breath. "I've been appointed as your defense attorney."

"You look awfully young. How many murder cases have

you defended?"

"None, but I've done extensive research in criminal law and there are a number of experts I can call on for assistance."

"I hope so because I expect you to get me off the hook," Dick snapped.

"I'll do the best I can," Dave assured him. "Now can you tell me what happened the night of the fire?"

Dick recounted exactly the same story he told the investigating officers. . . He had fallen asleep on the sofa and woke up when the house was engulfed in flames.

"I've read your file and the prosecution has a good case against you. It looks like your best option is to let me strike a deal with Stu Leonard for a guilty plea to the lesser charge of murder in the second degree. You'll get life, but seven to ten years down the road you'll be eligible for parole."

"Huh, that's my best option? No way. Try again."

"Well, you can always plead guilty by reason of insanity."

Dick's face reddened. "I'll do no such thing. I didn't start the fire and I'm not insane."

"Dick, let's review the facts. A few months before the fire, you took out a huge insurance policy on your wife."

"And one on myself, too. Don't forget that," Dick interrupted.

"You also bought the electric space heater that caused the fire," Dave continued.

"So what!" snarled Dick.

"The State's arson investigator will testify that the thermostat was removed and that caused the heater to overheat. That fact goes to premeditation and don't forget we're talking three counts of murder here."

"You can't prove I took that thermostat off the heater. Maybe there never was one on it."

"Oh, there was one all right. The signs of it having been removed are there, plain as day," Dave continued. "Your neighbors will also testify that they heard you and your wife arguing about money on numerous occasions and that you physically abused her."

"No law against that. The motel took every cent we made, there was never enough money to go round. Yeah, we argued about money. I could've told you that, you don't need testimony from my nosy neighbors and I did slap her around a few times."

"Then there were your actions the night of the fire. Instead of trying to save your family, you ran next door and asked for help."

"I've explained that a dozen times. I couldn't get to them because of the smoke and the flames. I ran to Rebecca Sutherland's house and asked her to call the fire department."

"Dick, as your attorney I'm telling you that your chances of being acquitted on these charges are slim and none."

"Yeah, well, I still won't plead guilty or insane."

"Let me remind you that Montana has the death penalty and that's by hanging."

Dick's right hand automatically went to his neck, his face blanched white. "I'll think it over," he whispered.

"Well don't think on it too long. I have a lot of work to do. First, I'm going to move the court for a change of venue. Sentiment is running so high against you in this town, I doubt if you could get a fair trial here."

"What do they say about me leaving Rocky Bluff?"

"At the time you left, the investigation was still open. No charges had been filed against you, nor were you a suspect. The prosecution will probably not try to draw any inferences from your departure. He really doesn't have to. He has all he needs to convict you without speculating why you left. Look, Dick let me try to plea bargain with Stu Leonard. He'll accept a guilty plea to murder in the second degree."

"You're my lawyer. You're supposed to have my best interests at heart. Why are you trying to get me to plead guilty?"

"I do have your best interests at heart, Dick. I'm trying to save you from hanging. Again let me remind you: The prosecution's case against you is overwhelming. I'll do my level best for you, but I still believe your best defense is to seek a plea bargain of a guilty plea to the lesser charge of second degree murder."

eleven

"Good morning, Rebecca," Principal Diaz greeted as Rebecca signed the school register that she was on campus. "How are things going in the library?"

"Great, but I have a lot of things to get done before the last day of school. The students are extremely slow in getting their books returned and I'm still working on the inventory."

"I'm sure everything will get done in the end," her principal assured her. "This is traditionally the most hectic time of the year for the librarian." He hesitated and took a deep breath. "I hate to ask you this on such a short notice, but I heard that you were able to play the piano."

A look of puzzlement spread across her face. "I used to play for personal enjoyment, but I'm pretty rusty. I haven't touched a piano since I came to Guam."

"I'm really in a bind," Mr. Diaz confided. "The band was going to play for graduation, but the band director has a death in the family and he left this morning for the mainland. There's only a week left before graduation and with the director gone the band is out. If you could play the piano for us at least we would have music. Could you play the processional for us?"

Rebecca paused, shrugged her shoulders and then nodded. "I suppose I could practice after school, and be able to have something worked up. It'll be far from perfect."

"No one will recognize perfection anyway," he grinned. "They're too excited with having their graduation before

Memorial Day. The public schools don't get out until the second week of June. We're trying it this way so our students will have first crack at the summer jobs."

"Sounds like a good idea. I'll look around the music room later today and see if I can find some appropriate piano music," Rebecca replied as she turned to leave the office.

After school that day Rebecca stayed in the music room and practiced traditional graduation marches. After an hour and a half she became tired and hurried home for a light dinner. As she walked down the hall she noticed the open door across the hall from her apartment and could hear the evening news on the TV.

"It's about time you're getting home," Ella Mae shouted. "Why don't you come in and have a cold drink with me?"

"Don't mind if I do," Rebecca replied. "We haven't had time to talk in a long time. How are things going at GW High School?"

"Busy as usual," Ella Mae sighed. "I'm glad the school year's about over. The kids are getting terribly restless. The hardest part for me is that Major Lee is going back to Georgia just as soon as school is out. GW won't be the same without him."

"You mean Ella Mae won't be the same without him," Rebecca teased.

The young teacher blushed. "Some of that, too. However, we plan to keep in touch. He wants me to come to Georgia to see him just as soon as I return to the States next summer. I don't know if we can sustain a relationship after a year of separation."

"I used to think the same thing," Rebecca admitted. "But I'm finding the longer I've been away from Andy the closer we're becoming."

"They say absence makes the heart grow fonder." Ella Mae jiggled the ice cubes in her empty glass. "By the way, your phone's been ringing off the hook this afternoon. Someone seems desperate to talk to you."

Rebecca shrugged her shoulders. "If it's important they'll call back."

The two continued their conversation for a few minutes and then Rebecca excused herself. Just as she was unlocking her apartment door her telephone rang again.

"Hello," she said, laying her purse on the kitchen table.

"Hello," a familiar male voice greeted her. "Where have you been? I've been trying to get you for the last two hours."

"Hi, Andy. I had to work late at school. It seems that the music teacher had to return to the mainland for a funeral and they didn't have anyone to provide music for graduation. Somehow the principal found out that I used to play the piano."

"So you were drafted?" Andy teased.

"Something like that. He somehow made me feel like it was my patriotic duty."

"That's what you get for being multitalented," Andy reminded her. He paused, cleared his throat, and took a deep breath. "Rebecca, why I called is there has been an important development in Dick Reed's case."

"What's that?"

"Dick is maintaining his innocence so there will be an emotional trial. Dave Wood, his attorney, filed for a change of venue because he didn't believe Dick could get a fair trial here. Judge Eubanks agreed and the trial has been moved to Great Falls. The trial is scheduled to begin July fifteenth. You'll be one of the primary witnesses."

"I was afraid of that," Rebecca sighed. "As much as I'll

enjoy coming home for the summer, I'm not looking forward to a long, drawn-out trial. I don't function well under pressure."

"I saw you handle the immediate fallout from the fire and you were brilliant. The trial will be a piece of cake in comparison. Just tell them what happened."

"I guess you're right," Rebecca shrugged. "I just don't want to have to relive those tragic hours again."

"It'll be tough, but I'll be there with you every step of the way."

"That's the most encouraging words I could hear. I've really missed being with you these last few months."

"Good," Andy chuckled. "Catch the first plane out of there when school is out and I'll meet you at the airport."

"The Blairs are comfortable in my house now and I promised they could stay there for two years so I'll have to find someplace else to stay."

"I suppose you know Beth's baby is due the end of June?"

"Yes. She wrote me the nicest letter. They're so excited and I'm delighted for them. They deserve the best. I wonder if Edith Dutton wouldn't mind if I stayed with her for a couple months."

"I'm sure she'd be pleased to have you," Andy assured her. "I'll talk to her tomorrow and explain the circumstances. When is your school out?"

Rebecca thought a moment. "Graduation's May thirtieth. I could be back by the third of June."

Rebecca could not see the broad grin that spread across Andy's face. "That's terrific. Our seniors don't graduate until June fourth. I'm sure Jay and Ryan would like to have you at their graduation ceremonies."

"Those two were among my favorite students. I watched them change from rowdy freshman into well-mannered young gentleman. I know they'll go far in life," Rebecca responded.

"Two weeks after graduation Jay is leaving for Lackland Air Force Base in Texas for Air Force basic training. He's so excited about seeing the world he can hardly stand it. However, his parents are having a problem letting him go."

"That's understandable," Rebecca replied. "The Harknesses have always been a close knit family."

The pair chatted for a few more minutes about the events in Rocky Bluff before they noticed the time and imagined dollar signs over the telephone lines. They hurriedly finalized their plans and bade each other good-bye, anticipating the time they would soon be together.

ॐ

"It's so thoughtful of you to bring me here to meet Rebecca's plane," Edith Dutton said as she and Andy Hatfield stared through the plate-glass window waiting for the evening Treasure State Airlines flight to arrive.

"You're the first one Rebecca wants to see," Andy replied. "Every time I've called her she's always asked about you."

Edith smiled as she remembered her former coworker at the high school. "We've shared our lives with each other, both the good times and the bad. I'm glad she'll be able to stay with me. We have a lot of catching up to do."

A speck appeared in the western horizon and slowly grew larger. The dozen people gathered in the Rocky Bluff Airport waiting room rose to their feet as the twin propeller, eighteen-seat Treasure State Plane rolled to a stop.

"The evening flying culvert has arrived," one of the men said as the others roared with laughter. Even though the small airline was the brunt of many jokes, everyone in rural Montana realized its existence kept them from sheer isolation.

As the door opened, Rebecca Sutherland was the third passenger down the steps. Tears filled her eyes as she gazed upon the snow-capped mountains in the distance. She was finally home.

As she walked into the terminal Andy grabbed her into his arms and held her tight. Their lips met before they realized where they were and Rebecca pulled away. "Andy, it's so good to see you. You don't know how much I've missed you."

"The feeling is mutual," Andy replied. "I've been marking off the days until you returned."

Just then Rebecca spotted Edith standing a few feet away and extended both her arms.

"Edith, thanks for coming. I've so missed all our heart-to-heart chats."

Edith hugged her longtime friend.

"I have too. I'm glad you're able to stay with me so we can visit undisturbed."

"How's Roy doing?" Rebecca queried.

"Not good," Edith sighed. "He's not able to feed himself anymore. He just lies on his bed barely aware when people come and go. Occasionally I can get a smile from him, but those times are becoming further and further apart."

Rebecca's smile faded. "I'm sorry to hear that. You both have been pillars of strength through extremely difficult times."

"I'll get your luggage," Andy offered. "How about dinner at the Steak House? I'm sure they don't provide meals on the flying culvert."

"They don't even provide peanuts," Rebecca giggled as the trio headed for the baggage claim.

Two nights later the Rocky Bluff gymnasium was filled with family and friends of the graduating seniors. Frances and Donald Reynolds arrived early in order to get a front seat in the special section reserved for family members. Their older son, Larry, and his family from Running Butte sat beside them.

"Mom, it looks like Ryan is up for a lot of awards and honors tonight," Larry whispered. "His athletic scholarship to Montana A&M will come in handy. Those are hard to come by. You must be mighty proud of him."

Mrs. Reynolds nodded. "We are."

"I'm sorry I let you down when I graduated. It must have been a terrible embarrassment for you."

Mrs. Reynolds took her son's hand. "Yes, it was," she admitted, "but now I'm bursting with pride for both my sons. You made your share of mistakes in your younger years, but you turned your life around after you made friends with the Harknesses."

"They're one terrific family," Larry replied. "I'd hate to think what would have happened to me if Edith and Bob hadn't intervened."

Three rows behind the Reynolds, Edith Dutton sat with her son and daughter-in-law.

"How does it feel to be father of the smartest kid in the class?" Nancy teased Bob.

"He must have gotten the brainy gene from you," Bob retorted, "or maybe it's a combination of you and Mother. It definitely didn't come from me."

Further back in the gymnasium, Rebecca Sutherland was crowded tightly against Andy Hatfield in the bleachers. His arm was lightly across her back to support her. Rebecca studied the program in silence. Each name was familiar as former students of hers.

"Hmm, this is interesting. Jay Harkness will be giving the valedictorian address," she whispered to Andy. "I'm not surprised that he obtained the highest grades in his class. He's always been an excellent student."

The fire chief chuckled. "You've missed all the town chatter. Having a valedictorian leave immediately for the military instead of college is an unheard of thing in Rocky Bluff."

Rebecca joined Andy in laughter. "I've always been proud of Jay. From the day he entered high school he's been his own person and thought for himself. Even when he was little he never gave in to peer pressure."

Andy shook his head. "Some people are caught in their own paradigm, thinking that the only way to get an education is to go to a four-year-college directly after high school."

Everyone rose as the band began to play "Pomp and Circumstance" and the senior class filed into the gymnasium. Dawn Harkness could scarcely play her saxophone as she kept one eye on her music and the other watching for her brother to come down the aisle.

Rebecca's eyes filled with tears as she thought about the changes she had seen in this class of students since she was librarian at Rocky Bluff High School. So much had happened to them and to herself during the last year.

The Harkness family stirred restlessly in their seats. Jay had refused to tell them what he was planning to say in his valedictorian speech.

"Jay's always been such a joker, I'm almost afraid what he'll say," Nancy whispered to her mother-in-law.

Edith patted her hand. "I'm sure we'll be proud of whatever he says. Jay knows when to tease and when to be serious. He's had a good set of parents."

Nancy smiled, relaxed, and leaned back in her chair. This was her son's big night. As class representative he was giving the farewell address to Rocky Bluff.

After the traditional introductory speeches, Principal Grady Walker took the microphone. "The valedictorian of this class needs no introduction to the community of Rocky Bluff. He has not only excelled in academics and athletics but has also worked in the family business and has volunteered for numerous community projects. I'm proud to announce the valedictorian with a three point nine seven grade point—Jay Harkness.

The roar was deafening as Jay walked to the podium. The clapping gradually subsided as Jay surveyed the crowd.

"Fellow classmates, teachers, parents, and friends," he began. "I feel extremely honored and humbled to stand here tonight as a spokesperson for my class. After thirteen years of being together it is now time to say good-bye to each other and go our separate ways. Some we may never see again. Others will be constant with us throughout our lives, but wherever we go and whatever we become, the community of Rocky Bluff, Montana, has given us a strong foundation. I'd like to say thank you to Mr. Walker, all the teachers and staff who have sacrificed of themselves for our entire class so that we would be grounded in truth, education, and the love of our country. Beyond that, I'd like to thank my family for being there for me when I needed them most. Many times I thought I could make it on my own but in the end I found security and strength in their faith and confidence in me. My parents, Bob and Nancy Harkness, taught me the importance of honesty and integrity that I see slipping away from our society in general. My grandmother, Edith Dutton, and her husband Roy have demonstrated to me that life is not merely for the young.

Education and love are intergenerational needs. I need the wisdom they have developed through their years of experience and I offer to them my youth and enthusiasm. When I become discouraged I need only remember my grandmother's struggle back from a near fatal heart attack and Roy's struggles today while he is convalescing in the care center. Even through their physical pain, they could find inner strength to go on and face an uncertain future, knowing God was in charge of their lives. I want to thank each one of them for my strong foundation as I leave Rocky Bluff to serve my country in the United States Air Force. I want to give back to society some of what has been given to me during my growing-up years in Rocky Bluff. Thank you and may God bless each of you."

The audience sat in stunned silence as Jay left the podium. *They must not have liked my speech,* he thought dejectedly. Suddenly a spontaneous round of applause began as everyone in the gymnasium stood to cheer the moving words of a young man wise beyond his years.

🐝

The next morning as Edith and Rebecca lingered around Edith's kitchen table after their last cup of coffee, their conversation was interrupted by the ringing of the telephone. Edith reached for the phone.

"Hello."

"Hello, Edith. This is Bonnie Jenson, the head nurse at the care center. Roy has taken a turn for the worse and I was wondering if you could come to the care center right away."

Edith's face blanched. "Is he all right?"

"He's having a little difficulty breathing, so we felt you'd like to be here."

"I'll be right there. Thanks for calling." Edith hung up

the phone and turned to her friend. "Roy has taken a turn for the worse and I need to get to the care center right away. Does Andy have the day off today?"

"Yes, he was planning on coming over later this morning. I'll give him a call," Rebecca replied as she reached for the phone and dialed the familiar number.

There was a flurry of activity in the Dutton home for the next few minutes. The two women hurriedly changed clothes, fixed their hair, and touched up their makeup. They were standing on the front steps waiting when Andy Hatfield's car pulled to a stop at the curb. Rebecca took Edith's arm as they hurried to the car. As Andy drove toward the care center each sat in their own silence, afraid of giving false hopes.

As the trio turned down the corridor toward Roy's room, Doctor Brewer and Bonnie Jenson were coming out of his room. Edith's eyes searched their faces for answers.

"How is he?"

"Edith, let's go to the family room and talk," Doctor Brewer said as he took her gently by the arm and led her to the nearby lounge. He motioned for her to be seated on the sofa by the window. "I'm sorry. Roy passed away about ten minutes ago. He did not suffer in the end, but closed his eyes and slipped away."

Edith sat motionless. Her nearly six years of happiness with Roy was over. Rebecca put her arm around her friend and pulled her close. Edith buried her face on her friend's shoulder and began to sob. All during Roy's long illness Edith had rarely shed a tear and now all the built-up pressures were released. Words were not necessary to share their mutual grief.

After ten long minutes Edith lifted her head, dried her eyes, and forced a smile. "Roy was such a good man, I'm thankful I was the one who got to share his latter years. Let's go to his room and say good-bye."

The three tiptoed solemnly into Roy's room. Edith took his lifeless hand in hers. "Farewell," she whispered. "I'll see you later. Thanks for a wonderful life together."

Edith turned to her companions. "I need to call Bob and Jean. They accepted and loved Roy as if he were their natural father. We'll need to contact relatives and make the final arrangements. Roy would want his memorial service to be one that brings glory to the God he loves. It should be a time to proclaim Christ's victory over death."

twelve

Sunday morning Edith awoke with a dull headache. It had been over a year since she had been awaking alone in her bed, but this day was different. She did not have the anticipation of going to the care center to visit Roy. For the second time she was a widow. The smell of freshly brewed coffee drifted into her bedroom. Edith wrapped her satin robe around her waist and ambled to the kitchen.

"Good morning, Edith," Rebecca greeted. "Can I fix you some breakfast?"

"Thanks, dear. A couple of pieces of toast is all I can handle now," Edith replied as she sank onto a kitchen chair.

Rebecca popped a couple of pieces of bread into the toaster and took a cup and saucer from the cupboard. "Did you sleep well?"

Edith shook her head. "I must have," she replied. "But I have a terrible headache that won't quit."

Rebecca surveyed her friend's wrinkled forehead. "Just take it easy today and I'll take care of the cooking and hostessing for your family and friends."

"Thanks. I'd appreciate that," Edith sighed. "Jean and Jim and Gloria will be here by noon. Usually Jean takes over the meals, but she's eight months pregnant and the summer heat has been bothering her a lot lately."

"I'll have everything ready when they get here," Rebecca assured her. "I may have to make a few hurried trips to the deli in the next few days."

Edith forced a smile. "I hate to put you in such a position," she murmured. "You're here as my guest. You shouldn't have to take care of my family, but I don't know what else to do. Nancy has always been a big help when I've needed her, but she has a houseful of relatives who came for Jay's graduation."

Rebecca spread butter and jelly on the freshly toasted bread and set the plate before Edith. "That's what friends are for. You've helped me during difficult times, and now I'd like to help you."

"I appreciate that. Since he's been ill for so long I thought I was prepared for Roy's death, but I wasn't nearly as prepared as I thought. All I want is to see him and talk to him one more time. I'm every bit as numb as when George died suddenly."

"I'm sure losing Roy has triggered all kinds of memories and emotions," Rebecca noted.

"That it has," Edith admitted, taking a deep breath. "Before I met Roy I never dreamed that I would ever be able to love anyone as much as I loved George. But I soon learned that love is different later in life. I learned to savor every moment we had together and took nothing for granted. The few years of joy I had with Roy makes the pain I feel now worth it all."

Rebecca nodded. "I'm glad to hear you say that. I'm beginning to wonder whether I should risk entering into a more permanent relationship later in life. No one could ever replace Eric."

"That's true," Edith reminded her. "Roy did not replace George, he complemented and added on to the relationship I once had. In fact, a second marriage gave me a second chance not to make some of the same mistakes I did in my younger years.

"Roy had so much maturity and depth of character. He'd

been through so much losing his first wife and having to raise a handicapped son by himself. His ability to forgive Bob for the car accident that killed his son was an example for the entire community. I'm really going to miss him."

Just then the back door slammed. "Hello, Mom," Bob shouted. "May I come in?"

"Come on in. The coffee pot's on."

"Nancy went to church with her family, but I wanted to spend the time with you. How are you doing?"

"I'm okay," Edith replied. "Everyone has been notified and the final arrangements have been made. Rebecca has promised to be hostess for whoever comes by the house."

Bob turned to Rebecca. "I don't know how I can thank you for all the help you've been for Mother. Your presence has taken a lot of pressure off the family."

"I'm glad I can help. You all have been a source of strength and encouragement to me throughout the years."

Bob stayed and reminisced with his mother about the good times he had shared with Roy. They talked about the beginning of the crisis center and how it had developed throughout the years.

As the clock tolled twelve noon, Bob stood and pushed his chair under the table. "Nancy and the others will be home from church soon. I better leave now and let you get dressed. You're going to be having lots of company this afternoon."

"Thanks for stopping," Edith replied. "Rebecca is planning dinner around six. I hope you can bring your family over."

"Certainly," Bob smiled. "As long as the commotion won't be too much for you."

❧

Wednesday afternoon Rocky Bluff Community Church was

crowded with family and friends wishing to pay the final respects to one of the patriarchs of their community. The service for Roy had much the same bittersweet grief as the funeral for his son had had six years before. Pastor Rhodes again reminded them that because of Christ's sacrifice, death no longer held a sting over them. The music comforted their souls as the soloist sang, "Because He Lives I Can Face Tomorrow." The service was a celebration of the life of someone who had fought a good fight and kept the faith until the end.

An hour later Bob took his mother's arm as they approached the gravesite in Pine Hills Memorial Cemetery. Roy was to be buried next to his son. Edith dabbed her eyes with a tissue. A lump built in Bob's throat. *I have to be strong for Mother, but no one knows how difficult it is for me to come back to this spot. It was here at Pete's burial that I realized how selfish and misdirected my life had become. I fought mother's remarriage every step of the way. And now, looking back, I'm so ashamed. Roy brought immeasurable happiness not only to her, but to the rest of the family as well. I hope I can lead a life of love and integrity until the end the way that Roy did.*

Six-year-old Jeffey Blair hurried past Edith and the rest of the Harkness family. In his chubby hand he clutched a long stem red rose. Solemnly he laid it on the casket.

"Good-bye, Grandpa Roy," he whispered. "I'll see you someday in heaven."

In the back of the crowd Andy Hatfield strolled across the lawn toward the gravesite with Rebecca Sutherland on his arm. "In spite of Edith's diminishing health and her tremendous loss, she's a pillar of strength," Andy noted.

"I've often wondered if marriage later in life is worth it when it's obvious that the human body is on a downhill slide," Rebecca replied, "but Edith has made it plain to me that mature love is stronger than failing health."

Andy nodded and chuckled softly. "They say loneliness is one of the greatest robbers of health among the elderly. Edith and Roy were a perfect example that love can lengthen your days on earth. As the days go by, I am beginning to experience moments of loneliness that I never felt as a young, active thirty-year-old."

Pastor Rhodes spoke the same words to the family and friends of Roy Dutton as he did six years before at Pete Dutton's gravesite. Choosing words from Paul's letters to the Corinthians and Thessalonians, Pastor Rhodes' voice echoed across the hillside:

"'Eye hath not seen, nor ear heard, neither have entered into the heart of man, the things which God hath prepared for them that love him.'

"'For our light affliction, which is but for a moment, worketh for us a far more exceeding and eternal weight of glory.'

"'For if we believe that Jesus died and rose again, even so them also which sleep in Jesus will God bring with him.'"

❧

A week after his step-grandfather's funeral Jay Harkness stopped by his grandmother's home to say good-bye before he left for basic training at Lackland Air Force Base in Texas. Edith and Rebecca relaxed on the sofa while Jay propped his feet on the chair beside Edith. Conversation flew easily. There was no generation gap as they exchanged their common interests and expectations. After half an hour Jay turned his attention to Rebecca.

"Tell me more about Guam. I've always wanted to see the tropics."

"It's a beautiful island with palm trees and sandy

beaches," Rebecca replied. "But a tourist will never know what Guam is all about. A person must live there and get to know the people and the culture and it will have meaning for them."

"How's it different? Aren't they U.S. citizens?" Jay queried.

"Yes, they are. The American flag is large enough to cover all types and cultures of people," Rebecca explained. "They are South Sea island people who have been thrust into the modern Western world in just three generations. Some have excelled in this new environment while others have become frustrated and have given up. Even the climate makes their attitudes different from us frozen Northerners. Their life-style is much more relaxed."

Jay sat entranced while Rebecca described the island and the people. "I'm glad there's an Air Force base on Guam. When I get done with basic training I'm going to put Andersen Air Force Base down as my first choice for assignment."

Rebecca laughed affectionately. "I hope you get it while I'm still there. I'd love to show you the island."

Jay stood and hugged his grandmother. "Good-bye, Grandma, I'll see you in eight weeks after I've completed basic training." He then turned his attention to his former librarian. "I hope the next time I see you it'll be in Guam." With that Jay disappeared out the front door to begin a new life.

༄

After two weeks of jury selection, July fifteenth finally arrived and the courtroom in the Cascade County Courthouse in Great Falls was packed. Stuart Leonard sat at the prosecutor's table with his paralegal, Libby Reynolds. In front of them was a laptop computer to record every word spoken and search for the context of any new laws that might surface.

Libby had worked for him in the Little Big Horn County Attorney's Office until her husband had been transferred to Running Butte. Stuart was never able to find a replacement of equal abilities and when the triple homicide case became time consuming he turned to his former employee. Libby worked closely with Stuart from Running Butte via fax and modem until she was totally familiar with the facts of the case and the laws involved.

Dave Wood sat nervously beside his client. He felt as if all eyes were upon him. *Whether I think Dick is guilty or not, he deserves the best defense possible. The outcome is up to the judge and jury,* he mused. *But how can I present a good defense when the supportive evidence is so weak?*

Rebecca Sutherland sat in the back row holding Andy's hand. "I don't know if I can go through with this," she whispered. "I've never been face-to-face with Dick since he was arrested."

"When you testify don't think about Dick, think about Anita and the two children. Remember, this is not your decision. Your only responsibility is to tell the facts as you know them and leave the rest up to the judge and jury."

Rebecca grinned as she squeezed her friend's hand. "Thanks. I needed that. I'm glad you'll be by my side during this entire ordeal to give me moral support."

Suddenly the side door opened and the bailiff entered the courtroom. "Please rise," he ordered. "The District Court of Cascade County is now in session. The Honorable Herman Kessler presiding."

As soon as Judge Kessler took his seat on the bench, he pounded his gavel and commanded. "You may be seated. The court will come to order." He paused. "The clerk will call the first case."

The clerk rose and monotoned. "The State of Montana versus Richard Reed."

Judge Kessler looked down at the prosecutor's table and asked, "Mr. Leonard are the people ready?"

"Ready, Your Honor."

He then looked to his right at Dave Wood. "Mr. Wood, is the defense ready?"

"Ready, Your Honor," Dave replied and then said. "Your Honor, I request that the rule be imposed."

Judge Kessler again turned to Stuart Leonard. "Mr. Leonard?"

"No objections, Your Honor."

"So ordered," Judge Kessler gaveled. "All persons who were subpoenaed as witnesses in this case will now retire to the witness room. You will remain there until you are either called or dismissed. You are ordered not to discuss this case with anyone."

A bailiff escorted Rebecca and Andy and the other witnesses from the courtroom.

Judge Kessler now directed his attention to the defendant: Richard Reed.

"Mr. Reed," he said as both Dick and Dave rose. "You are charged with three counts of murder in the first degree. As to the murder of Anita Reed, how do you plead?"

"Not guilty, Your Honor."

"As to the murder of Christopher Reed, how do you plead?"

"Not guilty, your honor."

"As to the murder of Richard Reed the Second, how do you plead?"

"Not guilty, Your Honor."

"Very well, your plea of not guilty is accepted."

With that Dave and Dick sat and Judge Kessler turned to Stuart Leonard. "Mr. Leonard, do you wish to make an opening statement?"

"Yes, Your Honor." Stu said as he rose and strolled to the jury box. Facing the jury, his opening statement of how the crime that took three innocent lives was perpetrated and how the state would prove the defendant committed the crimes was a masterpiece.

Dave Wood both admired and feared Stu's presentation. Dick Reed became visibly upset and whispered in Dave's ear. "Is it too late to cut a guilty plea for second degree murder?"

"I'll see what I can do as soon as Stu finishes his opening statement," said Dave, unable to conceal his disgust. *It's a little late for that,* he told himself.

When Stu finished and returned to his seat, Dave thought, *if this were not a courtroom, the audience would have applauded.* Judge Kessler interrupted his thoughts. "Mr. Wood, do you wish to make an opening statement?"

Dave rose and asked, "Your Honor, may we approach the bench?"

"You may," came the reply.

Dave motioned to Stu and the two lawyers quickly moved to Judge Kessler's bench. Judge Kessler was slightly annoyed. "Mr. Wood, this is highly irregular. What's going on?"

"Your Honor, my client wants to change his plea. May I have an hour's recess to discuss this with Mr. Leonard?"

"Mr. Leonard, any objections?"

"None, Your Honor."

"Very well." With that Judge Kessler gaveled his annoyance. "The court will recess for one hour."

The two lawyers and the defendant met in Judge Kessler's

ante room. "OK, Dave, you have the floor."

"Stu, Dick is willing to plead guilty to three counts of second degree murder and save the state the burden of a trial in exchange for a thirty-year sentence, ten years for each count."

"I don't consider this trial a burden, Dave. But I might agree to a plea of guilty of three counts of second degree murder in exchange for three life sentences. One life sentence for each of the innocents."

"But that means no chance of parole," said Dave.

"Take it or leave it," replied Stu.

"May I be alone with my client?"

"Sure," said Stu as he left the room.

As the door closed, Dick was furious. "You said you could swing it," he yelled. "You lied to me."

"I could have swung it back in Rocky Bluff before the court convened," Dave yelled back. "But you refused to even consider it. You are now facing three counts of murder in the first degree and Leonard will demand the death penalty. The choice is yours. I've done all I can do," said Dave as he sat down.

After a long silence a much subdued Dick said, "It beats hanging."

Dave rose from his chair, opened the door, and motioned for Stu.

"Well?"

"We'll take it," said Dave.

The three then entered Judge Kessler's chambers and explained the plea bargain they had reached. It was all over but finalizing the nitty gritty details, reconvening the court to officially change the plea, and setting a date for officially handing down the agreed-upon sentence.

&

Rebecca could not remember the dismissal of the court. She sat numbly in her chair as everyone filed out. As soon as the courtroom was empty Rebecca burst into sobs. Andy wrapped his arms around her and held her close.

"It's okay," he whispered. "It's over. We can now go back to Rocky Bluff and start our lives over again."

"I don't know why I'm crying. I knew how this was going to end. Seeing Dick and worrying about testifying was difficult, but I should have been able to handle it. I've had a year in Guam to fill my mind with new adventures and thoughts."

"Now when you go back you'll not have nagging questions and fears hanging over you," Andy reminded her. "You can approach a new school year with freshness and certainty which you never had during your first year on Guam. You can go back to Guam with the certainty that there is someone who loves you and is anxiously awaiting your return."

thirteen

The wind rustled through the pine trees as Andy and Rebecca strolled along Lone Mountain Trail to the peak of Old Baldy.

"Just think," Rebecca sighed. "In a week I'll be walking among palm trees instead of pine trees."

"It's going to be hard to say good-bye," Andy replied. "Nine and a half months without seeing you is just too long."

Rebecca nodded. "I know, but I'm bound to my two-year contract. Even if I wasn't under contract I feel honor bound to finish the library automation project."

Andy took Rebecca's hand as the trail became steeper.

"That's what I like about you the most," he said. "Your sense of dedication."

"I only do what I have to do. I'd much rather stay here in Rocky Bluff with you."

"This winter I'll have three weeks vacation coming," Andy said as he gazed into the distance. "I think I'll check with the travel agency about a round trip ticket to Guam."

Rebecca halted. A smiled spread across her face. "Do you really mean you'd come to Guam?" Her voice faltered. "I. . .I'd love to show you the sights."

Andy pulled her next to him. "I'd follow you to the ends of the earth."

"And you think Guam is the end of the earth?" Rebecca teased as she snuggled against him.

"It's sure a long way from Montana," Andy retorted as

his lips brushed hers.

As the pair reached the peak, they sat on a boulder to enjoy the view and a cold drink. Words were not necessary to share their mutual love and respect. They had both observed how rewarding love in later years could be by watching Roy and Edith Dutton. The same was happening to them, only their love had to grow over the distant seas.

ã

A week later Rebecca Sutherland stepped off the plane at the Won Pat International Airport. *I wonder if Ella Mae got my letter asking if she could meet me at the airport?* Rebecca wondered as she waited for her luggage in the baggage claim area. *If she's not here I guess I could call a taxi, but the taxis here are so undependable.*

In the distance Rebecca spotted her young teacher friend. Beside her was Major Tom Lee. She hurried to embrace her. "Ella Mae, I'm glad you could come. How are you? How was your summer?"

"I'm great. This was the best summer ever. Tom has returned to Guam."

Rebecca turned to the retired army officer. "Tom, it's good to see you again," she said as she extended her hand. What brought you back to Guam?"

"Love," he chuckled. "I went back to Georgia to work with my brother but construction on our new building was delayed for several months. I couldn't get this little southern belle out of my mind so I came back until Ella Mae finishes her contract at George Washington High School."

Ella Mae and Tom helped Rebecca carry her luggage to their car. "How about dinner at the San Francisco House before we go home?" Tom asked.

"Sounds good. The meals on the flight over were pretty

skimpy," Rebecca replied. "I want to catch up on all the latest news."

Within minutes the three were gathered in a corner booth in their favorite restaurant enjoying heaping plates of spaghetti with garlic toast. After a few minutes of small talk Rebecca turned to Tom who was sitting beside her. "So what are you doing with your time while you're waiting for Ella Mae to finish her contract?"

Tom squeezed Ella Mae's hand under the table as they exchanged knowing glances. "I'm a consultant for a local security firm. I've also been keeping busy planning our wedding."

Rebecca looked at Ella Mae quizzically.

Ella Mae nodded. "We're planning on getting married on Labor Day. We were waiting for you to get back so you could be my matron of honor."

Rebecca beamed. "This certainly has been a summer for romance. I'd be honored to stand up for you."

The rest of the evening the friends discussed wedding plans. As the sun began to sink over the Philippine Sea the trio headed toward their apartment building in Dededo. Rebecca unlocked the front door of her one-bedroom apartment and a flood of emotions overcame her. . .relief to be back on Guam was mixed with fatigue and a loneliness for Andy Hatfield.

৯

The morning sun was high in the tropical sky before Rebecca awoke. She showered and dressed and routinely walked to the kitchen. Reality hit her as she opened her refrigerator door. *What am I doing?* she scolded herself. *There isn't a bite of food in the house. I cleaned out the cupboards and refrigerator before I left for the summer.*

Rebecca grabbed her purse and walked to the parking

lot. *I'm glad Ella Mae was here this summer to drive my car occasionally,* she mused. *At least there's a good chance it'll start.* She unlocked the door and slid under the wheel. The scent of coconut air freshener greeted her nostrils. She chucked as she read the note taped on the steering wheel.

"Welcome Home." She turned the key in the ignition and the engine turned over on the first try. *What a dear to take care of my car this way,* she thought. *I've got to find a way to repay her.*

Rebecca turned off the side street onto Marine Drive and headed for McDonalds in spite of her dislike of fast food breakfasts. An egg sandwich sounded delicious. After eating alone Rebecca stopped at the neighborhood supermarket. Within an hour she was back at her apartment in Dededo. She spent the rest of the day recuperating from jet lag. Crossing the international dateline always left her body clock totally confused.

Late that afternoon Ella Mae knocked on her neighbor's door. "Rebecca, I need to go to the florists and pick out flowers for the wedding. Would you like to come with me?"

"Sounds like fun. It's been a long time since I helped plan a wedding."

The two friends laughed and joked as they drove to Pacific Florist in downtown Agana. In one week they would both be back at work and they had to take advantage of every minute. "What colors have you chosen for your wedding?" Rebecca queried.

"Pink and white. I want to use as many tropical flowers as possible. After we get back I'll show you the spot on the beach where we'll say our vows. We're planning an evening wedding to take advantage of the setting sun."

"It sounds beautiful. Are you inviting many guests?"

"Hopefully most of the faculty from George Washington

will be there," Ella Mae replied. Her eyes became distant before she continued. "I wish my parents could come, but it's too expensive and neither one of them could get the time off work."

"You'll have to have lots of pictures taken," Rebecca replied. "An island wedding will be a novelty for South Carolina. You'll be the talk of the town."

Ella Mae burst out laughing. "If you Yankees only knew how important romance was to those south of the Mason-Dixon Line you'd appreciate why I'm having the entire ceremony videotaped. It's liable to be shown in the local theater."

Rebecca joined her laughter. "If that's the case and I'm going to be a movie star, I'd better look my best. When we get done let's stop at Ardiss's Dress Shop and see if I can find a suitable bridesmaid's dress."

Before the sun set that evening every detail of the wedding that coming Saturday evening was finalized. The caterer agreed to provide a tent to shelter the wedding fiesta and guests who might linger long into the twilight hours.

The next few days flew by as Rebecca helped Ella Mae and Tom prepare their wedding. The day before the wedding the trio moved a few of Tom's personal belongings into Ella Mae's apartment in Dededo. At the end of the day they gathered in Rebecca's apartment to relax.

"I'm exhausted," Rebecca sighed as she collapsed onto her sofa. "Let's order out for pizza."

"I'm in favor of that," Tom grinned. "I'm tired myself and this will be the last time I'll see my bride before she walks down the beach tomorrow night."

୨୭

Nothing could have been more picture perfect than Major and Mrs. Tom Lee's wedding the following evening. The band played traditional island music before the ceremony and during the festivities that followed. Ella Mae was radiant in her white dress with a lei of tropical flowers around her neck and one clipped to her hair.

"The people of Abbeville will be talking about this for years," Rebecca teased as she hugged the bride.

At the reception, Rebecca spotted her friend and co-worker, Mitzi Quinata and her daughter Angela among the guests. She weaved through the crowd until she was beside them.

"Hello," she greeted. "It's good to see you again."

Mitzi embraced her friend. "Rebecca, I'm glad you're back on the island. How was your summer?"

"Extremely eventful," Rebecca smiled. "Sometime when we have a couple hours I'll tell you all about it."

"Have you been to the Academy yet?"

"I've been so busy helping Ella Mae with her wedding that I haven't had a chance. I'm definitely not ready for school to start Tuesday."

"It's been entirely repainted, both inside and out," Mitzi explained. "I never expected such an elaborate change."

"Did they do the library?"

"You wouldn't believe how much bigger it looks with white walls instead of institutional green."

"I can hardly wait," Rebecca replied and then turned her attention to the attractive young woman. "Angela, how are you doing? How was your summer?"

"I went to summer school at Guam Community College and took several basic courses," Angela explained. "I've decided to get a degree in cosmetology. I've always enjoyed trying to make people look their best. It lifts their morale and they walk away with their heads held high."

Rebecca put her arm around her former student's shoulder. "Good for you. I know exactly where I'll go when I need to have my hair done."

It was a magical night on Guam. Chamorros, statesiders, and Filipinos mingled together to celebrate the love of a young couple far away from home.

This was the true island spirit.

*

Airman Second Class Jay Harkness stepped off the Treasure State Commuter plane in Rocky Bluff. His eyes feasted on the distant mountain peaks. After eight weeks of Air Force Basic Training he walked tall and proud in his dress blues. He broke into a run when he spotted his sister, parents, and grandmother.

Jay picked up his sister and whirled her around. "Hi, Sis. Did you miss me?"

"Maybe a little," Dawn grinned. "It sounded impressive at school to say my brother's in the Air Force."

"I figured you'd milk it for all it's worth," he teased and then turned to his parents. He hugged his mother and kissed her on the cheek. Jay hugged his father who was proudly slapping him on the back.

"Welcome home, son. We're all proud of you."

"Thanks, Dad," he said as he looked at his grandmother beaming with pride. She looked older and more frail than what he remembered when he left. He gave her an extra long hug. "How are you doing, Grandma? I really missed you."

"I'm doing great, but life's getting pretty boring not having some kind of ball game of yours to go to," she chided.

The Harkness clan hurried to the baggage claim to pick up Jay's duffel bag. Everyone seemed to be talking at once. Jay had seen so much and had made so many new friends he was anxious to provide every detail of the last eight weeks.

"I've made your favorite meal," Nancy said as they

walked to their car on the far side of the parking lot.

"Roast beef with potatoes and carrots, I hope," Jay smiled.

Nancy took her son's arm. "I wouldn't fix anything else for your first night home."

The family lingered around the dining room table long after the last bite of apple pie had been eaten. They basked in each moment they were together as a family.

Bob waited through minutes of small talk before asking what was paramount on everyone's mind.

"Jay, how long are you going to be home?"

"Two weeks," he replied seriously, "then off to Maxwell Air Force Base in Alabama for twelve weeks advanced training. I've been accepted into computer services. When I complete that I'm being assigned to the Eight-O-Five Computer Services Squadron at Anderson Air Force Base in Guam."

Edith beamed. "You got exactly what you wanted. Rebecca will be thrilled."

"I hope nobody lets her know I'm coming," Jay responded. "I want the pleasure of surprising her face-to-face. I've already started corresponding with my military host and they've clued me in on what to expect."

A twinkle come into Dawn's eyes. "Guam? Mmm. You won't be able to take your car."

"Sorry, Sis. You'll have to give the keys back," Jay chided. "We're allowed to ship our cars. Remember that was just a loan we agreed upon."

Dawn shrugged her shoulders. "I know, but it was fun while it lasted. I've been saving money from my after school job and I almost have enough for a down payment on a car of my own."

Nancy turned to her son.

"What do you want to do while you're home? We'd like to spend as much time together as we can."

"I want to sleep a lot," Jay confessed with a grin. "Then I want to drive over to Montana A&M to see Ryan. His letters sound like things are going well for him there and he really likes it there."

"Would you like me to hold an open house for you Saturday night so all your friends can stop by and say 'hello'?" Nancy asked.

"Mom, that'd be super. It would save me a lot of running around. I'll get on the phone and let everyone know I'm back and that there'll be lots of food and soft drinks that night if they would like to stop by."

The lively family discussion continued for another hour when Bob looked over at his mother just as she was yawning.

"Getting tired, Mom?" he queried. "Maybe we should call it a day. I'll take you home if you'd like."

"I am getting a little weary," Edith responded as she pushed back her chair.

"Why don't you stay here, Dad," Jay offered. "I'll give Grandma a ride home. It'll give me an excuse to reclaim my car and see if I still remember how to drive."

"Now that's an unsettling offer," Edith teased as she walked toward the front door. "If there's a chance you've forgotten I'd rather ride with your father."

"Grandma, driving my own car is something I'll never forget," Jay responded as Dawn handed him the keys.

&

The next afternoon Jay Harkness stopped by the fire station to visit Chief Hatfield. Andy was just finishing some paperwork when Jay tapped on the open door.

"Jay, come in. When did you get back?"

"Yesterday afternoon. It's good to be back in Rocky Bluff. I see you're taking good care of it and it hasn't burnt down."

Andy grinned. "We did have a major grass fire at the edge of town while you were gone, does that count?"

"Not much," Jay retorted and then turned serious. "Have you talked with Rebecca Sutherland lately?"

"I called her Labor Day and she was doing great. She had just been matron of honor at a wedding on the beach."

"Sounds like fun," Jay replied. "Please don't let Mrs. Sutherland know until I get there, but I'm leaving in three months for the air base on Guam."

Andy could not mask his pleasure as he tried to visualize the island he had heard so much about. "Great. I'll get to have Christmas with you."

"But I won't be able to come home for two years," Jay protested.

Andy grinned even wider. "I know, but I already have my tickets bought for the winter holidays on Guam."

The dashing airman studied the face of the most confirmed bachelor in Montana. "Hmmm. This sounds serious."

"It could be," Andy replied. "If you can keep this quiet, I'll let you in on my personal secret."

"My lips are sealed."

"I'm going to take a diamond ring with me to Guam and present it to Rebecca at the exact spot where she was the matron of honor at the wedding. She described it as the most beautiful place on earth."

"Whoever said that love is only for the young was dead wrong," Jay laughed. "Those of you over fifty seem to have more fun with your romances than the young could ever imagine."

fourteen

I'm sure glad it's Friday, Rebecca thought as she shelved the last book of the day. *I'm ready for a day off, but ever since Ella Mae was married I've had a lot of free time that I've had to spend by myself.*

Rebecca flinched as the silence was broken by the creaking of the library door. A striking young airman in full dress uniform entered.

"May I help you?" she said as she left the stack and hurried toward the front of the library. Halfway across the room she halted. Her chin dropped.

"Jay Harkness?" she nearly shouted.

Jay opened his arms as he hurried toward her. "Mrs. Sutherland, I've never hugged one of my teachers before, but it's so good to see you."

"Jay, what are you doing here?" she gasped.

"I got my dream assignment, Anderson Air Force Base Guam."

"Congratulations! When did you get here?"

"Tuesday afternoon, but they've kept me so busy I haven't had time to contact you. I'm off for the rest of the day. How about going to dinner with me?"

"Sounds good. Do you have a place in mind?"

"Mrs. Sutherland, you're familiar with the island. Where would you suggest?"

Rebecca squeezed his hand. "Jay, now that you've graduated from high school you may call me Rebecca like all my other friends do."

"Thanks. I guess we'll have an entirely different relationship from now on," Jay replied. "Now, where should we eat?"

"I've always liked the San Francisco House. It specializes in every kind of pasta imaginable. It's quite a ways from here. Would you like to follow me?"

"That would probably be best," Jay replied. "I still get lost as soon as I get off the base."

Rebecca reached in her desk for her keys. "I'll lock up and be right with you."

Jay followed Rebecca's red Toyota down Cross Island Road onto Marine Drive and then into Agana. The excitement of the sights and sounds of island life entranced him. He wanted to see and do everything. He was more fortunate than other military personnel in that he had a familiar face from home to acquaint him with the island.

As Rebecca enjoyed a plate of lasagna and Jay devoured a huge order of ravioli, they updated each other on the events in their lives.

"It's too bad the Air Force sent you over just three weeks before Christmas," Rebecca noted. "It would have been nice to have another Christmas with your family."

"I know," Jay sighed, "but they needed someone in the position right away."

"Andy Hatfield is going to come for Christmas so you can have Christmas with us," Rebecca offered.

Jay bit his lip, knowing he had a secret to protect. "You and Andy need time alone together," he protested. "I don't want to be a third wheel."

"Jay, don't be silly. We Rocky Bluffers have to stick together when we're out of Montana. How about me showing you the island tomorrow?"

"If you wouldn't mind. There's so much to see. The

brochures the military gave me said that the southern part of the island is totally different from that around the base."

"You won't believe the difference," Rebecca replied. "Why don't you come to my apartment around nine o'clock? I'll make us some sandwiches and we can make a day of it."

"I'd love it. Before I leave base I'll stop by the commissary and get some ice and soft drinks."

The next day Rebecca took Jay to the same spots she visited during her introductory tour of the island. . .Talafofo Falls, Mount Lamlam, and the villages of Merizo, Inarajan, and Agat.

"Jay, I have a dear friend who lives just down the road in the village of Santa Rita. I'd love to have you meet her. I've told her all about the people of Rocky Bluff."

"Your friends are mine," Jay quipped.

Rebecca turned her car into a drive lined with banana trees. The cement house was a freshly painted white with green trim.

"Wait here and I'll see if she's home," Rebecca said as she slid from under the wheel.

Rebecca knocked on the screen door and within seconds a dark-haired Chamorro woman opened the door. "Rebecca, I'm glad you stopped by. Come in and relax. I just finished making a batch of cookies."

"I have a friend from Rocky Bluff with me who arrived this week for a two-year tour at Anderson Air Force Base. I'd love to have you meet him. He's a delightful young man."

Mitzi Quinata smiled as she looked over her shoulder at her daughter Angela. "Invite him in," Mitzi urged. "Maybe we could coax you both to stay for dinner."

Rebecca motioned for Jay to join her. He quickly obeyed

and Rebecca made the formal introductions. He politely greeted Mitzi and then turned to Angela. He blushed as he surveyed her natural beauty. For the remainder of the evening Jay's attention remained centered on the local girl who was studying cosmetology at Guam Community College. She was so different from the fair skinned girls he'd known in Montana.

༄

December twenty-third Rebecca was back at the Won Pat International Airport. She nervously paced inside the terminal as she waited for the plane from Hawaii to land. She watched the variety of races as they emerged from the covered ramp. Somewhere in the crowd would be her best friend from Rocky Bluff.

"Rebecca."

There trying to work his way through a group of Japanese tourists was Andy. As soon as he had broken through the crowd they were in each others arms.

"Andy, I'm glad you finally got here. I've missed you so."

"I've missed you too," he whispered as his lips brushed hers. "It seems like it's been forever since we were climbing Old Baldy together."

"Let's get your luggage and get out of here," Rebecca urged. "This place is too crowded for me."

Rebecca steered her Toyota toward her apartment in Dededo. Andy admired the waving coconut palms as they drove. "I always thought Hawaii was hot, but this is oppressive," he noted.

"What do you expect," Rebecca chided. "Look at the way you're dressed. I hope you brought lighter clothes with you."

"I don't own many light clothes," Andy replied. "Remember, I'm from Montana where there's now two feet of snow on the ground."

Rebecca laughed. "I'll have to take you shopping for Guamanian clothes tomorrow." She paused a moment and peered into the distance. "We're almost to the beach where Ella Mae and Tom were married. It's beautiful there. Would you like to stop?"

Andy beamed. This was almost too good to be true.

"Please do. Your pictures of it were beautiful."

As Rebecca parked her car under a coconut palm, Andy reached for a small box in his carry-on bag. They locked hands and began strolling toward the water.

"Your pictures didn't do this place justice," Andy noted. "I've traveled a lot, but I've never seen anyplace that could compare with this."

"I know. This is my favorite spot on the entire island."

The couple halted and Andy reached into his pocket and took out the small box. "Rebecca, I love you and I hope you will accept this."

She looked puzzled as she opened the box and then her face broke into a broad smile as tears welled in her eyes.

"It's beautiful," she whispered.

"Will you marry me as soon as you get back to Rocky Bluff? I've been so lonely without you."

Without hesitating Rebecca replied, "Yes, yes. Of course I will."

Andy took the quarter karat diamond ring out of the box and slipped it onto Rebecca's finger.

"It's a perfect fit," he said proudly.

The pair sat on the sand and watched the waves beat against the rocks. This was a sight so different from their home in Montana. Finally Rebecca looked at her watch.

"I've invited Jay Harkness over for dinner tonight," she said. "He was so excited about your coming."

"It'll be fun to see him again. I haven't seen him since he completed his basic training in Texas. How's he doing?"

"He loves the Air Force," Rebecca replied. "In fact, he was kind enough to arrange for housing for you with him at the base. It's beautiful out there."

"Thanks, I appreciate all you've done," Andy said as he took her hand.

Andy's vacation on Guam flew by. The happy couple viewed every part of the island. Jay was even able to convince him to try snorkeling with a group of his friends. Certain no one in Rocky Bluff would believe that their fire chief could possibly be that adventuresome, Rebecca was there with her camera to record the event.

The evening before Andy left Guam he and Rebecca returned to their favorite beach. "This is a memory I want to take back to Montana with me," Andy said. "I want to remember the wind blowing through your hair underneath a coconut palm with the sun setting over the ocean behind you."

"I'll always remember this spot, not because of Ella Mae's wedding, but because it's the spot where you asked me to become Mrs. Andy Hatfield. Up until Edith married Roy Dutton I never thought love over fifty was possible, but now I find it's even more precious than the first time around."

"I'll talk with Pastor Rhodes when I get back and schedule our wedding for the first open weekend in June. Don't worry about a thing. This will be a wedding ceremony planned exclusively by the groom."

❧

The weeks after Andy left passed slowly for Rebecca. She felt a tremendous sense of accomplishment as she looked around her workplace. The library automation project was winding down and the students were thrilled to be able to use the computer instead of their old fashion card catalog to locate their books.

During Easter vacation Jay called Rebecca early in the morning. "Rebecca, have you been listening to the radio?"

"No, I've slept in. What's up?"

"There's a typhoon warning and it's already at condition two."

Rebecca sat erect. "What does that mean?"

"It means that destructive winds are anticipated within twenty-four hours. The winds could be over a hundred miles an hour. Do you have any provisions set aside?"

"I've never given it much thought," Rebecca confessed. "I didn't think this was even typhoon season."

"It's not, but they say typhoons can happen anytime. Why don't I come and take you to the store? If you don't mind, I'd like to stay with you until the storm is over. I don't like the idea of you being there alone."

"Thanks, Jay. I appreciate your concern. I'll begin getting prepared for a water and power outage."

The next few minutes Rebecca spent filling the bath tub and every possible container with water. *How silly of me to live in the prime typhoon belt and not be prepared for the inevitable,* she scolded herself.

A sharp knock on the door startled Rebecca and she hurried to open the door. "Jay, come in. Thanks for caring. How do you know so much about what to do during typhoons?"

"The Air Force required everyone assigned to Guam to attend a special training session on typhoons. They directed that we do our best to look out for the civilian population, so here I am," he chuckled. "Come with me and I'll take you to the store. We don't have anytime at all to waste."

A light rain was already beginning to fall as the pair hurried to Jay's car. "Do you have a flashlight with batteries?" Jay queried.

"No," Rebecca replied meekly. "I've always relied on the electricity."

"Do you have a transistor radio with batteries?"

"No. I have an electric radio-alarm."

"Do you have enough canned food to last five days?"

"No. Most of my food is either fresh or frozen."

"Do you have candles or a hurricane lantern?"

"No. I guess I am in pretty bad shape."

"We can get all those things in Agana, but we're pushing our luck going shopping now. The stores are probably already packed with everyone looking for the same things," Jay noted.

Jay and Rebecca stopped at a combination grocery/variety store. They grabbed a cart and hurried down the aisles. They found everything they had talked about enroute plus a First Aid Kit and a manual can opener. Rebecca also bought a couple magazines from the rack along with a paperback book.

When they got to the checkout stands they found the lines halfway down the aisles. It took nearly twenty minutes before they were checked out. As they stood nervously waiting they could see the rain begin to pound upon the plate glass window of the store. The store owner locked the door so no one else could come in and then began pounding plywood over his windows.

As soon as Jay and Rebecca had paid for their supplies they snatched their bags and ran into the torrential rain. The windshield wipers could not clear the windshield fast enough as they inched their way toward Rebecca's apartment. They got soaking wet running from the car to the apartment.

"That will teach me not to be prepared," Rebecca said as she locked the door behind them. "I have a sloppy shirt and an oversized pair of shorts if you'd like to go to the bathroom and change."

"Don't mind if I do," Jay replied.

Rebecca rummaged in her drawers until she found what she was looking for. She handed them to Jay along with a towel from the hall closet. She then went back to the bedroom to find something dry for herself. She had no sooner gotten out of her wet clothes when the lights went out.

"I've never used a hurricane lamp before," Rebecca said as she rustled through the sacks. "But there's always a first time for everything."

She read out the directions of the newly-purchased kerosene lamp which came as a kit. "I'm sure glad we remembered to pick up the wooden matches. I haven't used these things in years. I wasn't even aware they still made them."

"It looks like we'll be roughing it for a while," Jay replied as he began going through the bags. "Let's turn on the radio and see what's happening. They update the warnings every two hours. It sounds like the wind is really picking up."

When they had finishing getting everything set up, Jay and Rebecca sat down to ride out the storm.

"Would you like a ham and cheese sandwich?" Rebecca asked. "We'd better eat them now because the refrigerator items won't be good much longer."

"Sounds good to me," Jay replied as he opened a couple cans of soft drinks.

As they waited through the storm Rebecca and Jay could hear the palm tree across the street crash to the ground, crushing a car in its path. Trash cans went flying past the living room window.

"Jay, we've been so busy getting ready for the storm that we didn't do the most important thing," Rebecca said as they pulled their chairs into into the corner of the kitchen away from the windows.

The young airman looked puzzled. "What's that? I think I've done everything the military class taught."

"We haven't prayed for God's protection."

Jay flushed with embarrassment. "You're right. After all Grandma taught me about prayer, I can't imagine I didn't stop to pray as soon as I learned there was a problem."

Rebecca and Jay took turns asking God for protection for themselves and for others on the island. The relaxing calm helped them refocus their thoughts and quiet their fears. They thumbed through the magazines to help pass the time and talked about the challenges of a Montana blizzard. They laughed at the irony of their conversation.

The night turned black as the wind began to subside.

"Maybe we should try to get some sleep," Rebecca suggested. "I'll get a pillow and you can stretch out on the sofa."

"I never thought I could sleep through a typhoon, but I feel secure in God's hand and I believe I could sleep for a week," Jay replied.

True to their expectations, they both slept soundly and did not awaken until the tropical sun was beating through their living room window. The apartment was unbearably hot as the electricity was still off and the air conditioner remained quiet in the window.

Rebecca pushed open the windows.

"The air is so heavy and humid," she said. "Even an electric fan would feel good now."

Jay stepped onto the patio. "There are power lines down all over the place. I don't think it would be wise to leave for the base yet. Turn on the radio and see if there's anything new."

Civil Defense Headquarters was still in control of the radio station and announced that all roads and streets were closed to vehicular traffic until further notice. Engineers from the Army National Guard and line crews from Guam Power were clearing debris and repairing downed power lines.

Jay picked up the phone. "The telephone lines are down as well. I guess you're stuck with me for a while longer. I can't even call the base to let them know where I'm at."

"If that's the case, how about some breakfast?" Rebecca replied, trying to sound cheerful. "How do cold breakfast turnovers sound?"

"Right now anything would taste good," Jay chuckled.

The morning passed slowly for the pair as they sat glued to their transistor radio. After what seemed like an eternity, the radio spread the good news that the emergency was over. Jay breathed a sigh of relief, said good-bye to Rebecca, and headed back to the base. The crisis was over, but the cleanup would last for weeks.

Guam Christian Academy suffered mild damage from the typhoon and several sections of the roof had to be repaired before the students could return to school. The added vacation made the days until Rebecca returned to Rocky Bluff drag by. She spent hours writing letters to Andy, Edith, and Beth describing the typhoon. Most importantly, she wrote to Bob and Nancy thanking them for raising such a thoughtful son. She explained to them how prepared he was and concerned for her safety. The Montana spirit was not confined within the state boundaries.

fifteen

After the students left on the last day of school, friends and colleagues packed the cafeteria of Guam Christian Academy for a Farewell Fiesta honoring Rebecca Sutherland. Friends from the other schools and her church joined the GCA faculty in bringing their favorite dish so the serving table had a truly international flavor. Each person came to say good-bye to Rebecca and wish her well. Everyone at school praised her for the library automation project.

Principal Diaz took the microphone and thanked Rebecca for her contribution to the school. He asked her to come forward and then handed her a plaque from the entire school honoring her for outstanding service.

Choking back tears, Rebecca struggled for words. "I'd like to thank each one of you for helping make this such a rewarding two years for me," she begin. "I feel that I have gained more by coming to Guam than I could ever contribute back. I'd especially like to thank Principal Diaz for his support and encouragement. Also, I'd like to say a big thanks to Mitzi Quinata who made me feel welcome the first day I walked onto the campus of GCA. There are many others who have meant a lot to me during my stay here. Among those Ella Mae and Tom Lee have made tremendous neighbors. I had the privilege of being matron of honor at their beautiful wedding on the beach."

Rebecca scanned the room and spotted Jay Harkness standing in the back with Angela Quinata. *They make a striking couple standing there. I wonder if their friend-ship will develop into something more,* she mused.

"I'd also like to thank a former student and friend from Rocky Bluff, Montana, for all his help. I hadn't the faint-est idea what to do during a typhoon and he stepped right in and walked me through the process. It was a humbling experience to have a former student teach me basic sur-vival skills. If any of you haven't met Airman Second Class Jay Harkness yet I'd encourage you to do so. From the day he stepped off the plane he fell in love with Guam and the island ways. He's the kind of person we can be proud of to represent and protect our country."

❧

That night Rebecca tossed and turned in her bed. It was a bittersweet time. She looked forward to going home to Rocky Bluff and Andy Hatfield, but she was leaving so many friends and memories behind. Early in the morning she gave her apartment key to the building manager and Ella Mae drove her to the airport. As the pair was walking to the terminal, a male voice behind her said, "May I help you with your bags?"

A shot of adrenaline raced through Rebecca's body. *I've been on Guam for two years without being assaulted, it can't happen now.* She wheeled around.

"Jay! What are you doing here?"

"Angela and I wanted to come and see you off. I'm sorry we're so late, but I was detained on base."

Rebecca took a deep breath and then grinned. "You gave me such a start. I'm so glad you're here. I didn't get to talk to you alone or say good-bye the night of my going-away fiesta."

"I wanted to let you know how much it meant to me having you here and teaching me the ropes of adapting to the Guamanian culture. Most of all I wanted to thank you for introducing me to Angela."

Angela blushed. "I've never made close friendships with statesiders before. I always thought they were rich and arrogant and looked down on us, but Jay is different. He appreciates the relaxed island flavor."

"I'm glad I got to come to Guam. I learned to appreciate the differences in cultures along with the similarities of all being one of God's creations. You and your mother were special people and I'll never forget you."

"I'll never forget you. I wanted to give you a going away present," Angela handed Rebecca a brightly colored box.

The four hurried inside and checked her luggage. While they were waiting Angela insisted that Rebecca open her package. Inside the box was a beautifully sculptured wooden clock the shape of the island of Guam.

"It's beautiful," Rebecca gasped. "I'll treasure it forever, but I've never seen this kind of wood before."

"It's ifil wood," Angela replied. "It's native to only this part of the world and is becoming very rare. It's so tough that it is often called iron wood."

The boarding announcement for the flight to Honolulu interrupted their well wishing. Rebecca hugged her friends and grabbed her present and carry-on luggage. Tears filled her eyes as she bravely walked toward her plane. The people of Guam were now a part of her history; she was soon to become Mrs. Andy Hatfield.

ɞ

The Treasure State evening flight taxied to a stop in front of the airport of Rocky Bluff Montana. An exhausted librarian entered the terminal. She had changed planes in Hawaii, Seattle, and Great Falls. It had been eighteen hours of flight time, not counting the three layovers.

Andy rushed toward her. "Welcome home," he whispered as he held her close. "I knew you'd be tired so I called Edith Dutton and she has a warm bath and a bed all ready for you. As soon as you wake up in the morning call me and we can begin making our plans then."

"Andy, you're so considerate," Rebecca replied as she laid her tired head on his shoulder. "You think of everything."

"I've never had a woman to take care of before and I think I'm going to like it."

When Rebecca arrived at Edith's, Andy carried her suitcase into the guest room and bade the two friends goodnight. Rebecca chatted a few moments with Edith and then both women went to bed early. Tomorrow would be soon enough for serious conversation.

The next morning it was after eleven o'clock before Rebecca walked into Edith's living room.

"Good morning," Edith greeted. "I trust you slept well."

"It was the heaviest sleep I think I've ever had. I feel great today and anxious to talk to everyone in town."

"Would you like some breakfast first?" Edith queried.

"Don't go to any extra trouble," Rebecca protested. "I can fix some toast and coffee for myself."

The two friends sat around the kitchen table talking while Rebecca ate her breakfast. After finishing she turned to Edith. "I think I better give Andy a call and let him know I'm up. We have a lot of planning to get done today."

"This is an exciting time for you," Edith noted. "Planning a marriage when you're over fifty is an entirely different experience. So much living goes into each decision."

Within minutes Andy joined Rebecca and Edith. "There's so much to do, I scarcely know where to begin," Rebecca said.

"Don't worry about a thing," Andy told her. "I've already done a lot of pre-work. First, where do we want to live? I assume you'll want to keep your home."

"You're right there," Rebecca nodded. "Since you were renting a small apartment it would be much more comfortable in my place. I need to talk to Dan and Beth Blair about their moving plans."

"Dan stopped by the fire station the other day and we had a nice long talk. He's been offered a job at the crisis center in Missoula and was all excited about the possibilities there. It's a much larger center and Beth will be able to work on a bachelor's degree. I don't know when they plan to move."

"I'll go over and talk with them later today," Rebecca replied and then turned to her hostess. "Edith, would you mind if I stay here for a few more days so the Blairs can have some flexibility in their moving plans?"

"I'd love having you for as long as is necessary," Edith assured her. "This house gets plenty lonely at times."

"Next question you're going to ask is about the wedding date. Right?" Andy teased.

Rebecca's eyes twinkled. "You're reading my mind."

"I talked with Pastor Rhodes and he reserved the church for June twenty-seventh. I hope the date's suitable. There were a number of weddings this month that he had to work around," Andy explained.

"The date's fine," Rebecca replied. "However, it won't give me much time to plan the details."

"I thought next week Edith could come with us when we drive to Great Falls and find you a wedding dress. I've already had the invitations printed so all we have to do is address them."

"You've thought of everything," Rebecca chided. "What

else have you planned?"

"Teresa Lennon agreed to plan the reception. She wants to know your colors just as soon as you get home. I've met with the florist and she's waiting for your final stamp of approval."

"Andy, you don't waste anytime at all do you?"

"I sure don't," Andy chuckled. "I've never gotten married before and if I'd known it would be this much fun I'd have done it a long time ago."

Rebecca grinned and shrugged her shoulders. "What else have you done?"

"Pastor Rhodes would like to meet with us a couple times before the wedding so I scheduled that for the next two Thursday nights," Andy explained.

"What about the rehearsal dinner?" Rebecca queried. "I suppose you've taken care of that as well."

"I didn't miss a thing," Andy replied. "I reserved the banquet room at Beefy's Steak House for twenty-five people the evening before the wedding."

Rebecca shook her head in amazement. "I suppose you even have the guest list prepared?"

"Only part of it," Andy replied as he reached for a tattered sheet of paper in his pocket.

Rebecca giggled. "It looks like you're going to invite half the town."

"I would have invited the rest of them but I don't know their names," Andy replied. "I also don't know the names of all your relatives."

"Looks like it's going to be a packed house," Edith inserted.

"That's what we want," Andy replied. "I want the whole world to celebrate with us." Andy suddenly became serious as he turned to Rebecca. "Kenneth and Laura Taylor were in town Memorial Day with Dick Reed's two children. They wanted to make sure their daughter's grave was decorated. When I told them we were getting married they were so excited. They plan to drive back for the wedding."

"How sweet of them," Rebecca replied. "After all their heartaches they're willing to come back and celebrate with us."

"The Taylors are tremendous people. They came through that tragedy with such grace and dignity," Edith said as she offered the happy couple another cold drink. "The children seem to be thriving under their care."

That afternoon Edith and Rebecca drove to Rebecca's home. As soon as they approached the front step the door was flung open.

"Rebecca, I'm so glad to see you," Beth exclaimed as she hugged her former boss. "Come and see little Edith."

A sense of peace enveloped her as she entered the living room. She was finally home. Across the room a dark-haired baby girl crawled toward them. Rebecca reached over and picked her up. "She's beautiful. She looks just like you." The baby babbled her satisfaction.

"Thank you," Beth beamed. "She's been such a blessing. Jeffey's so proud of her that he's become my number one babysitter."

Rebecca scanned her home. "Speaking of Jeffey, where is he?"

"He has a little league practice. He just loves it. He's going to be the next generation of Montana athletic stars."

"She's not exaggerating," Edith chimed in. "I went to his first game and he reminded me of Jay when he was that age."

"Dan contacted the Missoula Little League Association

and they have already assigned Jeffey to a team."

Rebecca put her arm around the young mother and pulled her close. "Beth, I'm so proud of all you've accomplished. I hate to see you leave Rocky Bluff, but I'm glad that you've decided to get a degree in library science."

"Thanks. I had an excellent mentor." A look of chagrin covered Beth's face. "I tried to have all our things packed and out of here by the time you returned, but the moving company can't come until the fifteenth. I hope that won't be a problem for you."

"No problem at all. Edith said I could stay with her until you're able to move. Andy and I were planning to redecorate anyway."

Baby Edith became restless in Rebecca's arms and reached for her mother. "I hope you both are free Saturday night," Beth said as she surveyed the two women. "I want to throw a big celebration party. God has been so good to us. Dan obtained a prestigious job in Missoula and I was accepted into the University of Montana. We're going to have our second anniversary this month and little Edith is having her first birthday on the twenty-third. Jean and Jim Thompson are going to bring little Heidi so we can celebrate their first birthdays together. Larry and Libby Reynolds are going to bring their children as well."

"I wouldn't miss it for the world," Rebecca assured her as Edith nodded in agreement. "That would be the best welcome home I could ever have."

The next few weeks flew by for Rebecca. She and Andy finished their wedding plans and changed the decor of her home to blend both their tastes. Former students dropped by her home, anxious to hear her tales of the South Pacific. But Guam seemed a hundred years ago and an entirely different lifetime. Her life now consisted of becoming Mrs. Andrew Hatfield.

A week before her wedding Rebecca was at the airport to meet her parents. "Mom, Dad," she shouted as an elderly couple walked through the door. "I'm so glad you could come."

"Honey, we wouldn't have missed it for anything," Charles Harris replied. "You've waited much too long to find yourself another love."

"I know," Rebecca grinned, "but Andy is well worth the wait."

"I'm anxious to meet him," Maud said as she embraced her daughter.

Charles Harris became serious.

"Rebecca," he began. "My Parkinson's disease has really been giving me problems and my walk has become so unstable. Could you find someone else to escort you down the aisle."

"I'll do no such thing," Rebecca protested. "I'll push you in a wheelchair if necessary."

Charles smiled. "Fortunately it's not that bad yet, but I just wanted to warn you."

"I'll tell you what, Dad," Rebecca suggested. "I'll take your arm as if you're escorting me. No one needs to be the wiser."

Tears filled Maud's eyes. "You've become such a sensitive woman, Rebecca. We're so proud of you."

"Thanks, Mom. Whatever I am is because of you and Dad."

☙

June twenty-seventh dawned bright and clear. The temperature hovered in the mid-seventies, a perfect Montana day. Early in the afternoon Rebecca drove to the church to help Teresa who was putting the final touches on the decorations in the fellowship hall.

"It's beautiful," Rebecca gasped. "You have such exquisite taste."

"I'm glad you like it," Teresa replied. "I'm so happy for you. Only you and Edith get an opportunity to have romance over fifty."

"I don't know about that," Rebecca protested. "I hear it's becoming more and more common. After I met Andy I realized that no aspect of life is limited to just the young."

Promptly at seven o'clock the organist in Rocky Bluff Community Church began to play the wedding march. There was scarcely a dry eye in the place as the maid of honor, Edith Dutton, strolled down the aisle carrying a bouquet of daisies. In the front she met the best man, Philip Mooney. The organist struck a chord and Maud Harris led the congregation in standing to respect the bride as she entered on the arm of her aging father.

Laura Taylor dabbed her eyes as Pastor Rhodes helped the happy couple recite the traditional wedding vows. He then addressed his words to the congregation, "Ladies and gentlemen, I'd like to present Mr. and Mrs. Andrew Hatfield. May their love continue to shine out to others proving that distance and heartache cannot dampen a love that is guided from above. May God bless them with a long, happy life together. Amen and God bless you."

Two hours later the congregation gathered on the church steps waiting the departure of the bridal couple.

"I hope I catch the bridal bouquet," Dawn giggled to her best friend.

"No, several of the girls who graduated a couple years ago are sure to catch it. Most of them have serious boyfriends and it's a toss up which one will be married first," the teenager replied.

A hush fell over the group while everyone reached for their packet of rice. Andy and Rebecca Hatfield stood at the steps and thanked everyone for their love and support. The single ladies giggled with anticipation. Rebecca tossed her bouquet toward them just as a gust of wind blew across the town. The bouquet drifted directly into Teresa Lennon's hands.

Teresa turned to Nancy Harkness beside her. "I'm glad I'm not the superstitious type. Otherwise I'd start getting nervous. I'm the most confirmed old maid in town."

A Letter To Our Readers

Dear Reader:

In order that we might better contribute to your reading enjoyment, we would appreciate your taking a few minutes to respond to the following questions. When completed, please return to the following:

Rebecca Germany, Editor
Heartsong Presents
P.O. Box 719
Uhrichsville, Ohio 44683

1. Did you enjoy reading *Distant Love*?
   ❑ Very much. I would like to see more books by this author!
   ❑ Moderately
      I would have enjoyed it more if _____

   _____

2. Are you a member of **Heartsong Presents**? ❑ Yes ❑ No
   If no, where did you purchase this book? _____

   _____

3. What influenced your decision to purchase this book? (Check those that apply.)

   ❑ Cover   ❑ Back cover copy

   ❑ Title   ❑ Friends

   ❑ Publicity   ❑ Other_____

4. How would you rate, on a scale from 1 (poor) to 5 (superior), **Heartsong Presents'** new cover design?_____

5. On a scale from 1 (poor) to 10 (superior), please rate the following elements.

    ___Heroine   ___Plot

    ___Hero   ___Inspirational theme

    ___Setting   ___Secondary characters

6. What settings would you like to see covered in **Heartsong Presents** books?_____

_____

_____

7. What are some inspirational themes you would like to see treated in future books?_____

_____

_____

8. Would you be interested in reading other **Heartsong Presents** titles?   ❑ Yes   ❑ No

9. Please check your age range:
   ❑ Under 18   ❑ 18-24   ❑ 25-34
   ❑ 35-45   ❑ 46-55   ❑ Over 55

10. How many hours per week do you read? _____

Name _____

Occupation _____

Address _____

City_____ State_____ Zip _____

Ann Bell

MONTANA

Rocky Bluff Chronicles

___*Autumn Love*—A bizarre incident at Rocky Bluff High School literally triggers Edith Harkness's retirement as a home economics teacher, and the start of her so-called golden years. Then Edith meets Roy Dutton, and the last thing she ever expected happens to her. HP66 $2.95

___*Contagious Love*—Despite the promise of Edith's joyous second marriage to Roy Dutton in the autumn of her life, life in this Montana hamlet is anything but blissful. Edith is drawn into a maelstrom of emotions and needs. Never before have her unwavering faith and contagious love been in such demand. HP89 $2.95

___*Inspired Love*—Beth Slater, a single parent of a four-year-old son, has a dream to cling to and the means to acheive it. That is, until now. For Beth to survive, she needs first to claim an inspired love—the love of her Heavenly Father—and then the love of a godly man. HP109 $2.95

___*Distant Love*—Although Rebecca is preparing to leave Rocky Bluff for a two-year position on Guam, she and fire chief Andy Hatfield team up to unravel the mystery surrounding a recent fire that has upset the close-knit community. HP137 $2.95

·····Heart♥ng ·····

Any 12 *Heartsong Presents* titles for only **$26.95** *

CONTEMPORARY ROMANCE IS CHEAPER BY THE DOZEN!

Buy any assortment of twelve *Heartsong Presents* titles and save 25% off of the already discounted price of $2.95 each!

*plus $1.00 shipping and handling per order and sales tax where applicable.

HEARTSONG PRESENTS TITLES AVAILABLE NOW:

_HP 3 RESTORE THE JOY, *Sara Mitchell*
_HP 4 REFLECTIONS OF THE HEART, *Sally Laity**
_HP 5 THIS TREMBLING CUP, *Marlene Chase*
_HP 6 THE OTHER SIDE OF SILENCE, *Marlene Chase*
_HP 9 HEARTSTRINGS, *Irene B. Brand**
_HP 10 SONG OF LAUGHTER, *Lauraine Snelling**
_HP 13 PASSAGE OF THE HEART, *Kjersti Hoff Baez*
_HP 14 A MATTER OF CHOICE, *Susannah Hayden*
_HP 18 LLAMA LADY, *VeraLee Wiggins**
_HP 19 ESCORT HOMEWARD, *Eileen M. Berger**
_HP 21 GENTLE PERSUASION, *Veda Boyd Jones*
_HP 22 INDY GIRL, *Brenda Bancroft*
_HP 25 REBAR, *Mary Carpenter Reid*
_HP 26 MOUNTAIN HOUSE, *MaryLouise Colln*
_HP 29 FROM THE HEART, *Sara Mitchell*
_HP 30 A LOVE MEANT TO BE, *Brenda Bancroft*
_HP 33 SWEET SHELTER, *VeraLee Wiggins*
_HP 34 UNDER A TEXAS SKY, *Veda Boyd Jones*
_HP 37 DRUMS OF SHELOMOH, *Yvonne Lehman*
_HP 38 A PLACE TO CALL HOME, *Eileen M. Berger*
_HP 41 FIELDS OF SWEET CONTENT, *Norma Jean Lutz*
_HP 42 SEARCH FOR TOMORROW, *Mary Hawkins*
_HP 45 DESIGN FOR LOVE, *Janet Gortsema*
_HP 46 THE GOVERNOR'S DAUGHTER, *Veda Boyd Jones*
_HP 49 YESTERDAY'S TOMORROWS, *Linda Herring*
_HP 50 DANCE IN THE DISTANCE, *Kjersti Hoff Baez*
_HP 53 MIDNIGHT MUSIC, *Janelle Burnham*
_HP 54 HOME TO HER HEART, *Lena Nelson Dooley*
_HP 57 LOVE'S SILKEN MELODY, *Norma Jean Lutz*
_HP 58 FREE TO LOVE, *Doris English*
_HP 61 PICTURE PERFECT, *Susan Kirby*
_HP 62 A REAL AND PRECIOUS THING, *Brenda Bancroft*
_HP 65 ANGEL FACE, *Frances Carfi Matranga*
_HP 66 AUTUMN LOVE, *Ann Bell*
_HP 69 BETWEEN LOVE AND LOYALTY, *Susannah Hayden*
_HP 70 A NEW SONG, *Kathleen Yapp*
_HP 73 MIDSUMMER'S DREAM, *Rena Eastman*
_HP 74 SANTANONI SUNRISE, *Hope Irvin Marston and Claire M. Coughlin*

*Temporarily out of stock.

(If ordering from this page, please remember to include it with the order form.)

•••••••• Presents ••••••••

Hearts♥ng Presents
Love Stories Are Rated G!

That's for godly, gratifying, and of course, great! If you love a thrilling love story, but don't appreciate the sordidness of popular paperback romances, **Heartsong Presents** is for you. In fact, **Heartsong Presents** is the *only inspirational romance book club*, the only one featuring love stories where Christian faith is the primary ingredient in a marriage relationship.

Sign up today to receive your first set of four, never before published Christian romances. Send no money now; you will receive a bill with the first shipment. You may cancel at any time without obligation, and if you aren't completely satisfied with any selection, you may return the books for an immediate refund!

Imagine. . .four new romances every month—two historical, two contemporary—with men and women like you who long to meet the one God has chosen as the love of their lives. . .all for the low price of $9.97 postpaid.

To join, simply complete the coupon below and mail to the address provided. **Heartsong Presents** romances are rated G for another reason: They'll arrive *Godspeed!*